Richard Carpent

Ro
SHE OD

FITZWARREN'S WELL
&
THE LADY'S CHOICE

Richard Carpenter's
Robin of Sherwood
Fitzwarren's Well
& The Lady's Choice
By Jennifer Ash
Published in 2025 by
Chinbeard Books

in association with
Oak Tree Books
oaktreebooks.uk

Editor: Barnaby Eaton-Jones
Sub Editor: Harriet Whitehouse

Cover art by Robert Hammond
With thanks to Lucy and Dennis Collin

Cover shows Judi Trott as Maid Marion,
Ray Winstone as Will Scarlet, and
Peter Llewellyn Williams as Much

Richard Carpenter's

ROBIN OF SHERWOOD

FITZWARREN'S WELL
&
THE LADY'S CHOICE

by

Jennifer Ash

A Chinbeard Books / Oak Tree Books Original

FITZWARREN'S WELL

by

Jennifer Ash

PROLOGUE

'Find me, Herne, Please find me.'

Marion sent a breathless plea into the trees as she ran, weaving through Sherwood in the early morning light.

Taking what comfort she could from the song of the birds above her, and the brush of a light spring breeze against her face, she ducked beneath a low hanging branch, before swerving to the left into a clearing between the trees. She'd barely taken two strides when an unnatural silence coated the air, stilling the trees and quietening the wildlife.

'Herne.' Marion slowed to a halt as the Lord of the Trees unexpectedly stepped forward and lowered his imposing stag headdress, appearing to her as a man—perhaps to show he understood her vulnerability.

'My son sent you to look for me, Marion of Sherwood.'

She nodded. 'He is too weak to come to you. They all are.'

Herne, gestured to a fallen trunk and sat down, tapping on the bark, indicating for Marion to join him. 'Tell me.'

Lowering herself to the makeshift seat, Marion felt some of the tension in her shoulders relax now that Herne had found her. She took a deep breath, clutching her hands together as she spoke, her voice laced with despair.

'Robin's head hangs low with pain… I just don't know what to do anymore… I've never seen sores like that on Nasir and Much. John's getting them too. He hasn't said anything, but I've seen him rubbing at his legs and arms when he thinks I'm not looking. And as for Tuck…' She paused, swallowing down her fear for her friends, '…Tuck can hardly keep his eyes open. I've tried everything I know—every herb we have—but his fever is burning out of control, and… they're afraid. I'm afraid.'

'Afraid that word will reach the Sheriff, and the Hooded Man's reign will end?'

Trying not to be disturbed by the sense that Herne's voice was somehow coming from far away, despite him being sat next to her, Marion said, 'They are too weak to fight… if the soldiers find us…' Her voice cracked as a tear ran down her face. 'Thank goodness Will's away visiting his brother, at least he's alright. At least, I hope he is.'

Herne inclined his head, his voice blunt. 'You are unaffected.'

'Yes.' Guilt made her heart constrict. 'What can I do?'

The breeze that wove its way between the trees picked up as Herne got back to his feet and replaced his headdress. 'Take my hand. Close your eyes.'

Doing as she was bidden; Marion couldn't help but flinch as she touched Herne's hand. 'You're so cold…'

'You can feel the water, Marion of Sherwood.'

'The water?'

Letting go of her palm, Herne spread his arms out and upwards, as if commanding the forest itself. 'Hear me and heed me. The one who calls himself Fitzwarren controls the Lady of the Well. You can't escape the heat without the cold. Two trials, by mind and iron, await before kindness is chanced. But the Lady will only help those who prove worthy.'

As he lowered his arms, Marion was surprised to see that a bag had appeared in his right hand.

'Take this. It holds all you need. Journey to the south of Sherwood. The path will take you to Beeston. Time is short.'

Accepting the proffered bag, Marion asked in confusion, 'Mind and iron? The Lady of the Well?'

'You will see.'

Marion blinked, not sure if Herne was moving away or simply fading in front of her eyes. 'But Herne, Beeston is almost a day's walk, and if time is short...'

'I will guide you, Marion of Sherwood. Go now; a scarlet blade approaches.'

CHAPTER ONE

Will Scarlet walked slowly, his usual lightness of step missing as he glared accusingly at his booted feet.

'I don't care how much John complains about the smell—as soon as I get to camp these boots are comin' off.' Weaving around a coppice of silver birch, he muttered to himself as he crossed Sherwood. 'Not much further, I can almost smell Tuck's cooking. Stew. I fancy some of his...'

The sound of a twig breaking sent his hand to the dagger at his belt. No sooner had he ducked beneath the cover of the trees, the hand was off his dagger and he was appearing again. 'Marion!?' he exclaimed, glad that it hadn't been a solder to be dispatched.

'Will! Oh thank goodness. Herne said I'd find you.'

Scarlet's forehead furrowed. 'Herne did?'

'Well, no, he said there'd be a scarlet blade. That had to be you.'

'What's going on?' Will scuffed a hand through his shortly cropped hair. 'Where are the others?'

'They're ill.'

'All of them?!'

'Yes. We've got to go to Beeston.'

'But that's miles away. I've just walked from Lichfield! My feet are killing me.'

Knowing she was close to tears; fighting to control her emotions, Marion looked her friend in the eye. 'We've got no choice Will! If we don't, I think…' She swallowed, '…Tuck might die, and I'm not sure about the others.'

'Die? Tuck?' Shocked, as much by Marion's exhausted expression as what she was saying, Will shook his head. 'No… he'll be fine. He's strong, they're all…'

Marion laid a hand on his arm, and spoke gently. 'Herne says they've been cursed.'

'Oh great!' Will grunted. 'Three days I've been walking. It was nice. No soldiers chasing me, no one to worry about, and no lunatics playing with sorcery!

Saw me brother at his pub and met a nice…' He let out a huge belch as if to prove a point, 'Well if I wasn't sober before, I am now!'

Rather than being annoyed by Will's self-centred response, Marion felt relieved by it. *At least I know Will is his old self.* She gave a half-smile, 'I wondered if you'd have a sore head when you got back. "Scathlock's serve the finest ale in Lichfield", wasn't that what Robin said the local sheriff's man claimed?'

Will snorted out a chuckle. 'Yeah, that's what they say. My brother 'as 'is faults, but he pours decent ale.' His belly rumbled, 'You got any food in that bag, Marion? If I've gotta keep walking, I'm gonna have to eat.'

'Maybe.' Rummaging inside, Marion explained, 'Herne said it held everything we need.'

'Let's get undercover and have a look.'

Following Will into the cover of the trees, Marion produced some food from the bag. 'There's some bread. Two loaves.'

'Herne did know I was coming then.' Will had long since stopped wondering how Herne knew what he knew. Taking a bite from the loaf Marion offered him, Will chewed as he asked, 'What else 'ave you got in there?'

'A water pouch… here…' Marion passed one to Will before looking back into the bag. 'Oh, and more pouches. They're empty.'

Will frowned. 'What's the point of that?'

Marion snapped, 'Well we've obviously got to fill them with something, Will!'

'Alright!'

'Sorry.' Marion puffed out a ragged breath. 'It's been so awful. Tuck got sick first, then Much, then the others. I've hardly slept trying to tend them. I've been so worried… and now I've left them to cope alone! What if some soldiers come and..?'

Heaving himself up off the floor, Will threw the remaining bread and the water pouch back into the bag. 'Then we'd better get going, ain't we? Give me that bag…' He threw it over his shoulder. '… and you can tell me everything that's been going on while we walk. Starting with what Herne told you, and who he thinks put this curse on 'em.'

Will had been lost in his thoughts for some time. The only sign that he was there was the occasional wince, as his boots chaffed his feet. It was almost midday before he spoke again. 'We're gonna face two trials?'

'That's what Herne said. One by mind and one by iron.'

Will scrubbed at his stubbled chin. 'So, I'll be fighting, and you'll be talking then.'

'Why can't Herne ever just say what he means?' Marion sighed wearily. 'There's more. We can't escape the heat without the cold, and the Lady—whoever she is—will only help those who prove worthy.'

'Right.' Will winced, as he stepped clumsily over a fallen trunk.

'You alright, Will?'

'Feet are covered in blisters.' Will's cheeks went uncharacteristically pink. 'Got new boots in Lichfield. Wish to hell I hadn't.'

Marion peered down at her friend's feet. 'So you have. Why? You've always had the same boots.'

'Yeah, well, time for a change…'

Marion laughed. 'You're blushing, Will!'

'No I'm not.' Will peered down self-consciously. 'I'm just cross about swapping me boots. The old ones fitted like gloves.'

'Yet, you bought new ones from a *lady* boot seller in Lichfield.'

'How did you know the boot seller was a woman?'

Marion laughed, not needing words to answer his question.

'Alright.' Will chuckled. 'I was on 'oliday weren't I.'

Marion kept in step with her friend. 'I'm so glad you're here. It seems ages since I laughed. If Robin doesn't get better, what will happen to the people of Sherwood?'

'Come here.' Stopping, Will opened his arms to her. 'I know I ain't Robin, but I'm told I give a decent hug.'

'By a female boot seller?' Marion rested her head on his shoulder.

'Yeah.'

Appreciating the sense of safety that filled her as Will held her close, Marion murmured, 'You should see Tuck, Will, he's so frail.' She paused to collect herself, pulling back slightly so she could see Will's face. 'When I was ward to Abbot Hugo, stuck in the castle with the Sheriff of Nottingham, all those years ago, Tuck kept me sane. Kept me going… We *must* help him.'

'We will. All of them.' Letting her go, Will gestured along the path. 'Come on.'

CHAPTER TWO

They'd crossed through several miles of forest before Scarlet asked, 'How will we know where to go once we reach Beeston?'

'Herne said he'd guide us.'

'Well let's hope he uses plain English when he does, or we might end up walking to Scotland.' He stared down at his new boots as he kept moving. 'God, my feet 'urt.'

Marion watched the shadows between the trees as they moved forwards. 'Herne said we'd been cursed by someone calling himself Fitzwarren.'

Will came to an abrupt stop. 'Fitzwarren? I heard that name in Lichfield.'

'You know who he is?' Marion rested her back against a tree trunk.

'Not exactly. It was a story. Ale talk over the fire. At least I thought it was…'

'Tell me.'

Will lifted his right boot up off the floor to relieve a little of the pain in his foot. 'Some balladeers came by the night before I left Scathlock's. It's probably a coincidence… but they sang of someone with that name.'

'So, it might *not* be him?'

'Maybe. Maybe not.' Will checked that no one was nearby. 'Let's sit down. It's safe enough under these trees. I need some water.'

Getting herself as comfortable as she could, Marion took the full pouch from her bag. 'Alright, but only for a minute. We must…'

'Keep going. Yeah, I know.'

'Here, have a drink.' Passing Will the pouch, Marion said, 'Tell me about this Fitzwarren.'

Gulping down some water, Will drew the back of his hand over his lips. 'He was a friend of King John—well, he was Prince John back then. Kids together they were, this Fulk Fitzwarren and John.'

'But something went wrong.'

'Don't it always! Well, Fulk, he found out that someone from up north was robbing rich folk while pretending to be him. He got angry about being blamed for stuff he hadn't done and so he murdered the robber—cut his head off, *and* the heads of his soldiers.'

Marion grimaced. 'That's horrible.'

'It gets worse. This Fulk was not pleased when, a few years later, King John gave the manor he expected to inherit to someone else—so he killed that 'someone else' too. Then Fulk lived as an outlaw for three years, before King John pardoned him.' Will scoffed, 'He would, wouldn't he? Posh old friends ain't they, living happy ever after.'

'You said it was just a story?' Marion took another sip of water.

'Yeah. That's what they said, but the thing is, the balladeers sang about us next. Are we just a story too?'

'Sometimes I wonder. Come on.'

Will reluctantly followed Marion's example and got to his feet.

'We've still got a long walk ahead.'

'Don't I know it!' Will tutted back a wince. 'Flippin' blisters!'

'You can take your mind off your feet by telling me about your beautiful boot seller.'

Will chuckled. 'How did you know she was beautiful? I never said what she looked like, did I?'

'Because I've known you a...'

'Long time? Yeah, so you have.' Will winked as he grinned at her. 'Rosanna, she's called. She's got this stunning pair of...'

Marion quickly interrupted. 'On second thoughts, maybe you should save this story for the others.'

'*Eyes*... I was gonna say eyes...'

Marion smiled. 'Of course you were, Will...'

The afternoon was beginning to cloud over as Will grumbled, 'We've got to be nearly there. This is the crossroads to London, but which way now? There's two roads and... three... no, four tracks.'

Marion considered. 'Can't be the roads. Can it?'

As if from far away, both outlaws heard the faint sound of Herne's voice. *'The path of blossom.'*

Peering down each of the four pathways, Marion was the first to spot a potential route. 'Blossom? Then it must be that one. Look, Will. Apple blossom.'

'It would 'ave to be the narrowest path, wouldn't it.' Will drew his sword as they moved forward. 'We'll have to go in single file. Stay close behind me.'

'Or you could stay close behind *me*.'

'And have Robin give me hell if anything happened to ya? Not likely!'

Keeping going, stooping low so they didn't knock the apple blossom off the trees, Marion said, 'I hope Fitzwarren isn't that one you were telling me about.'

'He probably ain't real.' Creeping forward, his sword at the ready, Scarlet suddenly stopped, and held out his hand. 'Wait.'

Marion stood stock still and whispered, 'What is it?'

'I can hear someone moving up ahead.' He took a single step forward, before stopping again. 'Quick! Get down…'

As Marion crouched down beside him, Will muttered, '…I can see someone. He's blocking another path.'

'It must lead to the lady that Herne spoke of.'

'Yeah.' Will narrowed his eyes, a feeling that something wasn't right nudging at his mind.

'What is it, Will?'

'Look at his face. There's something… he reminds me of someone.'

'Who?' Marion whispered.

'Dunno, but that smile, the way it…'

Marion felt a trickle of fear creep through her as she finished Will's sentence. '...only smiles on one side!'

Staring at each other in horror, the two outlaws mouthed the name of man they'd once had good reason to fear.

'Lord Edgar of Huntingdon!'

CHAPTER THREE

Patience had never been young Edgar Fitzwarren's strong point. In the past, each and every member of his family had commented on it—but not his friends, as he didn't have any. Friends only got in the way of ambition—and Fitzwarren was a very ambitious man.

Pacing back and forth across the entrance to the path which, ultimately, would lead petitioners to the Lady of the Well, Fitzwarren had long since abandoned any pretence at being content to wait for his quarry.

'Where is she? Hood's woman should be here by now.'

Spinning on the balls of his feet, he was about to pace in the opposite direction when he came to an abrupt stop.

'Unless she became ill too… No, no, I was careful. The Lady promised she'd spare Marion until she got here.'

Deciding there was no point in wearing himself out by patrolling an empty trackway, Fitzwarren sat down, resting his back against the trunk of an ancient oak tree. Stretching out his well-padded limbs, he yawned.

'Maybe she isn't coming at all. Maybe the Lady got it wrong—or lied to me.' Suspicious, he looked back along the path. 'Father told me never to trust women.'

Fitzwarren mimicked his father's rather clipped voice, 'Women just slow you down, son…' before yawning widely. Closing his eyes, he could see his father now—sat before the fire, waiting to tell him the news that would change their lives forever.

'Women just slow you down, son. They simply spend your money and add decoration to a room. Take my advice, use them when you need them, but never trust one.'

'Yes, Father.' Edgar Fitzwarren held his hands up

before the fire that crackled in the grate. Its heat blushed his cheeks red as it filled the manor's hall with a welcome warmth.

Lord Edgar nodded to a servant who had appeared to fill his wine goblet, before gesturing to the seat next to him.

'Sit down, Edgar. I want to talk to you about your cousin.'

'Robert?' Fitzwarren sat as bidden and looked expectantly at his father.

'Yes. My nephew, rumour has it, has turned outlaw.'

Fitzwarren was torn between amazement and horror that his cousin should abandon an earldom for a life of crime and hardship. 'Outlawry? Like Fulk Fitzwarren, Father?'

'Not exactly.'

Lord Edgar's eyes sparkled, but his expression remained thoughtful as he passed his son a goblet of wine.

'Fulk risked outlawry for a matter of principle. A risk that paid off.' The elder Edgar snorted derisively, 'Robert, it seems, has answered a calling. He has gone into Sherwood to do *good*.'

'Whatever for, Father?'

'Apparently he feels *sympathy* for the people.'

Taking a drink, possibly to wash the taste of such a disagreeable concept from his mouth, Lord Edgar stared into the fire. 'You never knew his mother, but she was nice to everyone. He probably picked the habit up from her.' He paused, fixing his son with an unblinking stare. 'I trust you'd never do anything so futile?'

'No, Father!'

With a sharp nod of approval, Lord Edgar continued. 'Your cousin's foolishness, however, has made me think. As you know, I have two brothers, the King of Scotland and, Robert's father, the Earl of Huntingdon.'

Fitzwarren was about to speak, but just a glimpse of his father's expression told him he'd be unwise to interrupt.

Taking another drink, Lord Edgar looked back towards the fire. He spoke carefully, mindful of the servants attending to their tasks around the hall in which they sat.

'I feel it is my duty to provide you, Edgar, with a better inheritance. One more deserving of the name Huntingdon than this meagre manor. I have a plan… a way to use your cousin's foolishness against him.'

Fitzwarren sat forward, 'A way to increase my lands—our lands?'

Shuffling closer to his son, Lord Edgar inclined his head. 'David, Earl of Huntingdon is a powerful man. He has some sway over the Crown—but King John is *my* friend, and I know him to be wary of my brother. Especially now Robert has started to call himself Robin Hood.'

'Robin Hood?' Fitzwarren was astonished. 'But I've heard of him, Father. There are stories. The people...'

'The people are stupid.' Edgar of Huntingdon banged his fist against the table, silencing his son. 'As I was saying, the king is keeping a close eye on my brother now. It wouldn't take much to sow seeds of doubt in his direction.'

As understanding dawned, Fitzwarren gave a sly smile. 'And have the earldom passed to us—you—instead?'

Privately applauding his son's ill-hidden ambition, Lord Edgar continued with a quiet determination. 'My plan will take time to arrange, but it is sound. However, Hood is not without friends, and he is loyal to his father. He might try to stop me. If Robert succeeds—which he won't because I intend to ensnare him in his very own trap—but if he does somehow stop me... then you *must* work to get the earldom for yourself.'

'I won't have to, Father, because you *will* succeed.'

'Yes.' Toasting his similarly-named son with his goblet, Lord Edgar smiled wider. 'Yes, I will. If loyalty to the Crown is worth anything, then it is already ours by right!'

Sitting back to let a servant throw another log onto the fire, father and son sat for a while, each lost in his own dream of powers, until Lord Edgar asked a question that took Fitzwarren by surprise.

'Tell me, Son, do you believe in witchcraft?'

'No, Father!'

'Good, because it's nonsense. But the King believes in it. And that is going to prove very useful to us. Very useful indeed...'

CHAPTER FOUR

'You were wrong about witchcraft, Father. The magic in this realm runs deep. But I'll keep my promise. I'll get the earldom we deserve.'

Getting back to his feet, Fitzwarren kicked a stone off the path and into the trees. 'Robin Hood hides from justice, while I…'

His words melted into the air as he heard footsteps approaching. Drawing his sword, Fitzwarren was certain it would be her—the woman he'd been told would come. That at last, he could start to avenge his father's death.

A second later, his certainty faltered. 'Two of you?'

Marion felt cold as she confronted the man before them, his resemblance to his father taking away any doubt as to who his forebears were. 'You thought I'd come alone?'

Will scowled. 'He thought you'd have to, Marion. He thought I'd be cursed like the others…'

'And he waits with a drawn sword to greet a lady. What a gentleman!' scoffed Marion.

'Like father, like son!' Lunging forward, Scarlet's blade met Fitzwarren's with a solid clank.

Quickly realising he was no match for the outlaw's swordsmanship, Fitzwarren pushed Will away and leapt backwards, out of range. 'You know me?'

'You're a Lord's son.' Will spat out.

'And proud to be.' Fitzwarren replied.

'Yeah, you look just like that wasted excuse of a man.' Will added, grimacing.

Fury replaced the split second of doubt that had crossed Fitzwarren's mind. 'Don't you dare presume to judge me or my father! *You*, who works for my father's killer!'

Marion rested her hand on the handle of the dagger she kept in her belt, as she regarded the man blocking their way. 'Robin didn't kill your father! He fell from his horse. Robin told me.'

'He was hardly going to tell you the truth, was he!' Bitterness etched Fitzwarren's reply.

Scarlet rolled his eyes. 'You're as mad as Edgar

was. He accused the Earl of Huntingdon of *witchcraft*—his own brother! Just so he could get his hands on the earldom!'

Marion stifled a yawn. 'What do you want me for?'

Fitzwarren observed her with a smile. 'Getting tired, Lady Marion? A little achy perhaps?'

Glancing at Will, Marion said, 'What? No, I'm fine. It was a long walk, that's all.'

'No sores on your arms or legs? No headache brewing?'

'No... I'm fine, thank you.'

Fitzwarren's lips curled into a lopsided smile. 'Are you sure?'

Marion staggered to the left, letting out a cry of pain as she steadied herself against a tree.

Will dashed to her side. 'What have you done to her!?'

'Nothing at all—except to make sure the curse cast on every outlaw in Sherwood didn't reach her until she reached me.'

'You ba—' Will broke off as a strange sound reached his ears.

Weakly, Marion held onto his side as an ethereal humming floated towards them, as if being carried on the wind. 'Will, listen...'

Fitzwarren chuckled as the eerily musical melody grew louder. 'The Lady of the Well grows impatient.'

Will snarled, 'Who is this lady?'

'The Lady guards a well of the purest water. Drinking from it is the only thing that can lift the curse she placed on every outlaw in Sherwood.'

'But what've we done to upset 'er?' Will wrapped an arm around Marion's waist.

Fitzwarren's reply was smooth. 'She does not like killers.'

'You steaming great hypocrite, you…'

Marion raised a shaky hand, 'Scarlet wasn't in Sherwood when the curse was cast and I… I just have a headache. Hardly unusual.'

'Is that all? Are you sure?'

'I…'

Fitzwarren laughed as he saw Marion rest more heavily against her friend. 'You *will* persuade Robert of Huntingdon to forfeit the earldom to me—the *rightful* heir. If you do that, the lady will lift the curse and you and your friends can recover.'

Will was furious. 'You scum… you…'

Again, Marion interrupted. 'You did all this to get me here. Cursed my friends to the point of death, just to secure a power you aren't entitled to.'

Anger gripped Fitzwarren. 'Says the disgraced daughter of Huntingdon's best friend!'

Determined to show no evidence of the headache that was trying to persuade her eyes that they wanted to close, Marion enquired, 'If you feel like that about me, how do you know I won't just pretend I'll persuade Robin, so you'll lift the curse, and then not do it?'

'Because the Lady will watch from the well to make sure you keep your part of the bargain. And if you don't...'

In one stride, Will was at Fitzwarren's side, his face inches away from the man who blocked their path. 'Tell Marion how to find the well that lifts the curse! NOW!'

Will had struck Fitzwarren's sword before he'd finished speaking.

Parrying, Fitzwarren yelled, 'Not until she agrees to speak to Hood!'

Fighting in earnest this time, Fitzwarren focused on the blade that swung expertly before him,

Marion winced as the clash of metal on metal, and the thudding of boots against the forest floor, made her head pound worse than ever—a rumpus that was underscored by the strange singing that was slowly—stealthily—getting louder.

Will swiped his sword against his opponent's blade with extra force. 'Pathetic! Hoping you'd have a woman alone to fight.'

Unruffled by the insult, Fitzwarren blocked Scarlet's attack. 'Why waste energy I might need to get what's rightfully mine?'

'If you thought a sword fight with Marion would be easy—even when she's ill—then you're a bigger fool I took you for.'

As Will upped the pace of the fight, Fitzwarren began to wheeze with exertion. Seconds later, Will administered a perfectly constructed blow, and Fitzwarren's sword fell from his hand as he dropped to his knees.

'As I thought. All mouth and no fight.' Will sneered at his opponent with contempt. 'What's your name anyway? I ain't calling you Huntingdon—you don't deserve the title.'

'Edgar… like my father…'

'I don't care to call you his name much either.'

'No matter. I prefer…' Groaning on the floor, the fallen man mumbled, 'I prefer you call me… Fitzwarren.'

His suspicions that this was the man Herne had warned Marion about, Will tapped the end of his sword against his cheek. 'Well then, Fitzwarren, tell me how to help our friends or I'll cut your useless sword hand off.'

'You wouldn't dare!'

'You wanna find out?'

Relieved that the fighting had stopped, Marion stepped forwards. 'How do we lift the curse?'

Fitzwarren shrugged off his defeat with a triumphant grin. 'You don't. Only the lady can do that.'

Will poked Fitzwarren in the chest. 'Don't you dare give Marion one of your creepy smiles! You've lost!'

'Lost? How can I have lost? Your fight hasn't even begun yet.'

Kicking Fitzwarren in the shin, Will was about to give him a piece of his mind, but Marion stopped him. 'Listen.'

The haunting hum faded as, faint and far away, a female voice, floated on the air towards them. 'Marion of Sherwood… approach the well.'

'That must be her, the Lady of the Well.'

Will looked anxiously at Marion. 'You can't go down there on your own. I'll come too.'

The Lady of the Well sent an immediate reply. '*Just* the Lady of Sherwood.'

Not questioning how the Lady had heard them,

and privately cursing anyone who used magic to get one up on them, Will tapped an ill-fitting boot irritably against Fitzwarren's leg. 'I'll guard this excuse for a human being, Marion. Be careful.'

'Thanks, Will.' Marion let go of her friend and turned to face the path from which the haunting song was drifting. 'Herne said I can't escape the heat without the cold… the heat must be the fever, so perhaps the well water is cold? So…'

Her words broke off as the strange song morphed into the gushing of running water. Two steps on, and Marion's hands came to her head. Pain shot through her as she gasped, turning back to see her friend. 'Will! My head… I…' She gulped, gasping as she dropped a hand to her throat. '…can't breathe… I…'

Marion's cries merged into the wail of water that rushed towards Will. He stepped forwards, reaching out a hand to her… but Marion had disappeared.

Panic filled Will, as he stared at the spot where she'd been, only seconds before. 'Where've you gone? Marion! I can't see you.' He rounded on Fitzwarren, his sword at his throat. 'Why can I hear water when there isn't any? Where he she?'

Taking no notice of the blade, Fitzwarren laughed as the thunder of the water increased.

Will swung around as he heard Marion's terrified voice crying out to him. 'Will! It's so cold…'

'Marion! Where you?'

'Will…'

Marion's voice faded into the echo of a cascade of water that no one could see.

CHAPTER FIVE

Marion's legs felt unsteady as she rose to her feet. She could still hear moving water, but it was gentler now—lapping. Yet, as she looked about her, there was no water to be seen.

'Move slowly, Marion of Sherwood.'

A breathless Marion searched for the source of the voice, but there was no one there. It was only then that she realised she was no longer freezing, nor were her clothes, hair, or skin wet.

'I'm dry? But I was underwater… It was so cold. I thought I was drowning.'

Taking no heed of Marion's confusion, the Lady's voice rang out, clear but curt. 'You have travelled the path to the realm of the well. What do you want of me?'

'I am here to beg your kindness, my Lady. May I fill some pouches with water from your well to cure my friends?'

The Lady appeared from out of the shadows. 'And what makes you think they are worthy of curing?'

Marion curtseyed in the presence of the stunning woman, with golden hair and a silken gown, which shimmered as if it was made of water. 'Many rely on us. The people of Sherwood would starve if we didn't help protect them from the sheriff and the injustices of the Crown.'

'Words like that are easily spoken. Yet, I have good reason to believe you worthy of the curse laid upon you.'

Marion's head thumped anew as the Lady of the Well came nearer, her blue and green dress swishing like the flowing of a stream as she moved.

'What good reason?' asked Marion, frowning.

'My guardian—he came to me; distraught, broken—deprived of all that was his. Robbed of his future inheritance. By Robin Hood.'

Marion watched as the Lady swirled around and walked through a thickly planted group of trunks. Following her on shaky legs, Marion gasped as she found herself in a small glade, surrounded by beech trees—in the very centre of which was a circular stone well.

Only when the Lady had reached the centre of her domain did Marion protest. 'Robin has done none of those things!'

'You lie!' As the Lady cried out, the water splashed violently within its confines of the well.

'I tell the truth. Fitzwarren isn't even your so-called guardian's real name. His name is Edgar, and he is the son of Lord Edgar of Huntingdon, the younger brother to the Earl of Huntingdon and the King of Scotland.'

'I know well who he is! He changed his name to protect himself. To stay hidden from you and your friends!'

Shivering with cold, still feeling as if she was soaked to the skin despite being bone dry, Marion pleaded, 'Please my Lady, he has misled you.'

'He has not!' Circling to the other side of the well, the Lady placed her palms on the stone wall. 'He tells me truthfully that he is cousin to the one they call Robin Hood. The man *you* love, Marion of Sherwood. The man who murdered Fitzwarren's father.'

'No! I mean—yes, he *is* Robin's cousin, but there was no murder.' Marion reined in her emotions as she remembered that she needed the Lady's help. 'Lord Edgar fell from his horse. It was an accident.'

The water within the well stirred restlessly as the Lady shook out her yellow hair. 'Fitzwarren has proved worthy. As my guardian, he was sworn to protect me. Why would I believe you and not him?'

'Because Robin Hood is not like Lord Edgar, or his son. He is a good man who helps others. He…' Marion stopped talking. She rubbed her head, puzzled. 'My headache. It's gone. I feel better.'

'You are near the well now. There is no sickness here. No weakness of the body.'

Marion smiled, relieved as she felt her strength returning and the cold receding. 'Thank you, my Lady.'

Her visitor's gratitude took the Lady by surprise. 'You thank me, although I have refused to help you.'

'But you *have* helped me. Calling me to the well has made me better.'

The Lady observed Marion with more interest. 'The power of the well only lasts while you are within its realm. Unless you drink from its waters, once you leave here, you will be weakened by the curse once more.'

Marion signed. 'But we've done nothing to you?'

‘Cursing you was Fitzwarren’s request, and his reward, for guarding my path.’

Observing, as the water in the well stirred restlessly, Marion tried again. ‘But my friends, my Lady, they…’

The Lady gave a sharp tut, breaking off Marion’s entreaty. Then, picking up a stone, she threw it into the well. The water leapt high, before spinning like an angry whirlpool.

‘The well shows me death. I know who this Robin Hood is. I know the loyalty of his men. So much death in their wake. In *your* wake—Marion of Sherwood.’

‘But…’

The Lady pointed a slender finger towards the water as she commanded, ‘Look into the well!’

Stepping forward, Marion frowned as the water suddenly calmed.

‘It looks so still, but it sounds as if a storm is raging.’

‘The water responds to my thoughts and to the deeds of those around it.’ The Lady ran a hand through her long hair. ‘See how it reacts to you, Lady Marion. Your friends will get no help from me.’

CHAPTER SIX

Tying Fitzwarren's hands behind his back, Will Scarlet shoved his adversary against a tree. Warning him to stay put, unless he wanted to be secured to the beech's trunk.

'*Iron and mind*... well, I've done the iron bit—that has to have been the fighting.' Will muttered to himself as he stood guard over his prisoner. 'If you can hear me, Herne, protect Marion for me.'

'Go on, appeal to that forest spirit of yours!' Fitzwarren scoffed. 'See what good it does you. And you call *me* pathetic!'

Giving Fitzwarren a kick, Will snarled, 'If Marion don't come back, walking down that path in five minutes to us, then *we're* going after 'er.'

Fitzwarren shook his head. 'Only those who are

called may go down the path to the well.'

'Yeah? We'll see about that…' Will began to pace up and down the short stretch of path before him. 'How did you know of this place anyway?'

'Wouldn't you like to know!'

'Yes, I would!' His temper naturally short, Will felt it fraying at the edges. 'And if you don't want some of them ribs cracked, I suggest you tell me!'

'Alright, alright!' Fitzwarren tried to shuffle further away from Will but was prevented from moving by the trunk behind him. 'I've been living in Scotland with my uncle. He agreed I should go to Huntingdon to persuade the Earl to pass the earldom to me.'

Will was furious. 'That title belongs to Robin! When the time comes, he…'

'He'll turn it down and stay in Sherwood! You know he will! My father *was* next in line to the earldom—until Robin Hood killed him.'

Although Will didn't want Robin to leave Sherwood, knowing Fitzwarren was probably right about Robin never returning to Huntingdon didn't improve his temper. 'How many times do we have to explain this? He didn't kill him!'

Seeing that Will was about to kick him again, Fitzwarren, pleaded, 'Please! No!'

Lowering his leg, Will growled, 'Then answer my questions! How did you find the Lady of the Well?'

'I heard a tale about a magical well from a traveller at an inn near Chesterfield.' Fitzwarren spoke fast. 'After buying them a few ales, I discovered that the Lady of the Well—who could both curse *or* cure—was more than a story. So, I took a detour.'

Will threw him a look of pure distaste. 'And I guess when you got to Beeston, you flashed that half-smile at everyone until they told you all about her?'

Fitzwarren merely shrugged. 'I like stories, and this one hadn't reached my ears before.'

Moving away to check that there was no one hiding in the trees or approaching them along the pathway, Will muttered to himself. 'Nor mine.' Only when he was satisfied that they were still alone, did he return to Fitzwarren. 'How did you find the Lady?'

The nobleman dipped his head in the direction of Beeston. 'The barmaid in the tavern was talkative.'

'I bet she was!'

Fitzwarren looked smug. 'Seemed we had the same liking for evening strolls.'

Will let out a humourless bark of laughter. 'And she led you here. Telling you all about how to reach the Lady of the Well.'

'Yes.'

'Then you planned how the Lady could help you get the earldom without getting your 'ands dirty.'

Suddenly angry, Fitzwarren peered down his nose at his gaoler. 'I prefer to use my brain before my fists. You should try it sometime!'

Will gritted his teeth, only just stopping himself from knocking a few of Fitzwarren's from his mouth. 'The Lady of the Well? She curses people *and* cures them?'

'She'll only curse those who a petitioner can prove unworthy, and only cure those whose existence is worthy of saving!'

Will narrowed his eyes. 'How did you persuade her that our lives were less worthy than yours?'

Fitzwarren tilted his chin upwards as he grinned. 'Maybe she likes my smile...'

'...and then there was the time when Robin saved the future Queen of England from traitors.' Marion couldn't help but smile at the memory. She had been afraid at the time—afraid that they would fail in their quest to protect Isabella of Angouleme, or that the man who'd pretended to be Arthur of Brittany would kill Robin—but now, all she felt was pride. 'I promise you, my Lady, my friends have saved many lives; fought so much injustice. Robin Hood took an oath to help the weak and helpless—and he keeps that oath every single day.'

The Lady's gaze levelled on the water contained within the circular stone wall. 'You speak passionately…' She threw another stone into its depths; instantly the water ran faster. '…yet the well shows me bodies.'

Marion did not deny it. Sorrow chimed in her voice as she explained, 'Every soldier, every innocent man or woman that gets hurt or killed as we fight… we don't forget them. Each death is regretted.'

Suspicious, the Lady stated, 'And Lord Edgar of Huntingdon; is his death regretted?'

'Yes, by his brother and his nephew.' Marion kept her eyes on her companion. 'Robin told me how upset his father was when they found Lord Edgar's body. And, considering Edgar had tried to have the earl beheaded for treason, that shows what a good man Robin's father is.'

'Perhaps.' The Lady paused for a moment, before adding, 'But, you say no more than I'd expect. Women in love should support their men.'

Marion watched as the water in the well became as still as a millpond. Not sure how to convince the Lady to unlock the curse, she was unable to keep the sense of defeat from her voice. 'But it's all true, it's...'

Raising a hand to silence her petitioner, the Lady pushed her shoulders back as she came to a decision.

'Marion of Sherwood, I challenge you to a question and a riddle. If you fail to satisfy me with the answer you give, you will leave here uncured, to die a cursed death. If your answer satisfies me, you will be granted enough water to revive your friends. Do you accept the challenge?'

Surprised, Marion answered quickly, before the Lady could change her mind. 'Yes, I accept...'

A furious thunder of water resonated from the depths of the well, a sound accompanied by a weighty thud as, as if from nowhere Will Scarlet and Fitzwarren landed in a heap next to it.

Marion rushed towards her friend in alarm. 'Will! What's happened? Why are you here?'

'To help you, of course! This miserable retch has tricked her into helping him.'

The Lady's pale cheeks burned crimson. 'How dare you come uninvited into my realm?'

Jumping to his feet, his teeth chattering with

cold, Will ignored her as he turned to Marion. 'Why ain't I wet? There was water and…'

Fitzwarren interrupted, with a smooth smile playing on his face as he talked. 'I'm sorry, my Lady. My hands were tied—literally.' He gestured to his tethered wrists. 'This outlaw—*her* companion—dragged me here. He wouldn't listen.'

'Of course I wouldn't listen! You sent Marion into danger without a thought, just to secure riches for yourself.'

'Don't be a fool, Scarlet. *Not* just for myself.' Fitzwarren sneered as he bowed towards the beautiful woman standing by the well. 'Untie these ropes for me would you, my Lady?'

CHAPTER SEVEN

Marion's hands came to her hips as she looked directly at the Lady. 'You and Fitzwarren? Of course! "Women in love should support their men."—it makes sense now. No wonder you wouldn't believe that Robin didn't kill Lord Edgar. You're in love with his son!'

The Lady put a hand into the well's rushing water, as if to soothe it, as she gestured to the ropes she'd so recently taken from her lover's wrists. 'Tie up your newfound friend, Edgar.'

Marion felt all the progress she'd made with the Lady fade away. 'That's why you won't listen to the well, even though you hear how the water rages.'

Not wanting to accept what she was hearing; the Lady strode towards Will. 'It is you and *this* scruffy rogue that the well doesn't like!'

'Who you calling 'scruffy'?' hissed Scarlet.

Marion spoke over him, 'But, my Lady, it was calm until…'

Cutting off Marion's protest, the Lady reminded her of their agreement. 'You said you'd accept my challenge.'

Will was wary. 'What challenge is that, then?'

'Be quiet, outlaw!' Fitzwarren bellowed, 'The Lady is not talking to you.'

Ignoring the menfolk, the Lady stepped closer to Marion. 'My question is this. How many more will suffer in your quest to help others?'

'More than we would wish. But more lives will be lost if we stop what we do.'

'An honest answer.' The Lady inclined her head in approval.

'Marion always answers honestly!' Will snapped.

A second later, he was regretting speaking, as Fitzwarren took the chance to get his revenge, and kicked him hard in the leg.

'Ahhh!!'

'I told you to be quiet, outlaw!' As Fitzwarren yelled at Will, the water in the well swelled.

The Lady raised an arm towards Marion. 'I am asking this riddle of you alone, Marion of Sherwood—just you. No other may answer.'

Marion nodded.

'What connects the Prisoner in the Dark, the King on his Throne, and the Lady of the Well?'

Will closed his eyes, muttering under his breath. 'Come on, Marion, Herne's set us enough riddles in the past. You can do this…'

Watching the erratic flow of the water, Marion mulled the question over to herself. 'The Prisoner in the Dark, the King on his Throne, and the Lady of the Well. Hmmm. Not a possession, then. For a prisoner has nothing…' She paused, to mull it over, and then the pieces started to fit together, 'Nothing that can be held, nothing that can be stolen… so…'

It felt like time was standing still. To Marion, she was thinking as fast as she could, trying to connect the dots to make the picture form in her head. For Will, it was a matter of life and death, which felt like an eternity. For Fitzwarren, any time spent watching Marion try to decipher, meant that she was failing. And, for the Lady, time meant nothing. And everything.

Marion suddenly hit upon something. 'It has to be a feeling…'

The Lady tapped a hand against the well's stone wall. 'I require an answer Lady Marion.'

'But there are so many emotions.'

Fitzwarren sneered, 'For every second you waste, Friar Tuck slips further from this world.'

Marion suddenly smiled. 'Fear! The answer is fear!'

Fitzwarren, glowered at the outlaw. 'How dare you imply the Lady of the Well could ever be afraid?'

'Hush, Fitzwarren.' Placing a hand on her lover's arm, the Lady turned her blazing blue eyes upon Marion. 'Explain your answer to me, Marion.'

Doing her best to ignore Fitzwarren, Marion spoke clearly, 'A Prisoner in the Dark would be afraid of many things—torture, hunger, death. A King on his Throne would also be afraid of many things—treachery, assassination, uprisings. And you, my Lady of the Well, here in your realm... you must be afraid too. Afraid that, one day, no one will come. You are afraid of being alone.'

An eerie silence coated the glade. Even the water in the well stopped moving.

Hiding the shiver of unease that tripped up his spine, Will realised what Marion was saying. 'And your story is dying... the tales of you dwindle. They must be, or we'd have heard of you before, my Lady.'

Moving away from Fitzwarren, the Lady returned to the side of the well and let out a sorrowful sigh. 'I've sent many men from Beeston to tell my tale, in payment for saving their parents or cursing a landlord. So few return. They find new lives with new work elsewhere, forgetting why they left—until their loved ones become ill. Then back they come, asking for help.'

'Leaving you alone, month after month.' Marion felt a familiar tug of sadness. 'Resentment at their lack of gratitude—their unworthiness—festering inside you.'

When the Lady did not respond, Marion continued more gently. 'And that's why Edgar is here. Why you ignored the well's warning—so you'd never be lonely again.'

Fitzwarren opened his mouth to protest, but Will got in first. 'Let me guess. Edgar 'ere came, armed with his smile, and promised he'd keep you company.'

The water in the well began to move again, trickling droplets over its sides… as if it were crying.

Marion shot Will a 'get ready' look, before facing the Lady. 'It isn't Will or me the water was warning you about, but him.'

Fitzwarren's palm was wrapped around the handle of his sword as he leapt towards Marion. He hissed into her defiant face. 'She is to be my bride.'

The well water surged.

Will, struggling against his rope bindings, tutted in disbelief. 'Oh, so you're giving up your claim on the earldom to live here then, are ya?'

'Once she is my wife and I'm an earl, I'll visit her often.'

'Rubbish! You'll get what you want and forget her.'

Marion saw the Lady's face blanch at the implication. 'Will's right, my Lady. I'm sorry, but he is.'

'They lie!' shouted Edgar.

'Silence!' The Lady held up her hand. 'Wait by the path, Edgar.'

The nobleman hesitated, his forehead knotting in concern. 'You aren't going to listen to them, are you?'

Pushing her shoulder's back, the Lady of the Well addressed Fitzwarren with a serenity that Marion suspected she was battling to maintain. 'I wish to speak to our visitors alone. You swore to guard the pathway forever. So guard it!'

As Fitzwarren stalked away, the Lady returned to the well. 'You may take water to cure your friends, Marion. But *only* them—no others. Only those *I* decide worthy may drink from the well's waters.'

'Thank you, my Lady.'

The Lady rested her palms on the side of the

well and let out a low slow breath, before moving to Will's side and freeing his wrists. With a nod of thanks, Will took the water pouches from the bag as the Lady drew Marion to one side.

'I've been a fool. I'm sorry for your friends' suffering. You may both drink from the well to renew your strength before your journey back to them.'

Marion gave her a kind smile. 'You have been tricked in the cruellest way; you are not to blame. What will you do now?'

A hint of menace came to the Lady's voice as she stared towards the gap in the trees which led from her glade to the pathway beyond. 'Teach him a lesson.'

Knowing Will would disapprove of what she was about to suggest, Marion lowered her voice. 'Perhaps you should let him go.'

The Lady regarded Marion in amazement. 'He had me curse you and your friends, but you'd have me show mercy to him?'

'His father set a bad example.' The memory of Lord Edgar's gloating face made Marion shiver.

'Very well. If it is your wish. I will give him one chance. If Edgar answers a question honestly, he can leave here.'

'And if he doesn't?'

'The well can have him.'

EPILOGUE

The roar of the water within the well drowned out the stamp of Fitzwarren's angry pacing, as he marched back and forth in front of the Lady.

'I can't believe you let them go! After all the trouble we went to, to get Marion here! They haven't sworn to get Hood to plead my case to the earl yet!'

'Nor will they.' The Lady pointed towards the water. 'Look into the well, Edgar.'

Taking no notice of the Lady, Fitzwarren continued to stride back and forth, muttering to himself as he moved. 'I suppose you could curse the earl instead, but my uncle wouldn't be pleased. And it's not wise to upset the King of Scotland, so...'

The water became increasingly restless as the Lady spoke, each word full of bitter regret. 'I was blinded by the chance for love. The well told me I'd been duped, but I didn't want to believe it.' Tilting her neck up, she ordered, '*Look into the well.*'

Fitzwarren came to an abrupt stop. Suddenly nervous, he blustered, 'There is no need. I gave you my word!'

The Lady's blue eyes blazed. 'You told me these people's leader had killed your father and had destroyed more lives than they'd saved—but that wasn't true.'

Fitzwarren shuffled awkwardly from one foot to the other. 'Well, no, but I meant what else I said—I love you! We'll marry. I'll visit every month. You could come to Huntingdon with me, but…'

'But I can't leave my realm.' She shook her head. 'How blind I've been, and how very convenient that very blindness was for you, Edgar.'

Seeing he was about to protest, the Lady hastily added, 'I have a question. If you answer to my satisfaction, you can leave.'

Fitzwarren kept one eye on the billowing water within the well. 'What question? What are you talking about? I can come and go as I like. You gave me the freedom of the realm—you said…'

'Silence!' The Lady clapped her hands together. 'You will answer my question.'

Fitzwarren gave a silent nod.

'You are named Edgar of Huntingdon, yet you call yourself Fitzwarren. Why did you choose that name to hide behind?'

Fitzwarren's unease dissolved in an instant. 'If only all questions were so easy to answer. I named myself for Fulk Fitzwarren—who, like me, was robbed of his birthright by another nobleman.'

'I know the story.' The Lady's smooth forehead creased as she regarded him. 'You took his deeds as your own?'

'The sentiment of them, yes. Fulk Fitzwarren fought for what was his. He is a hero!'

The last vestige of hope that, maybe he was a good man after all, evaporated. With a heavy heart, she said, 'A hero who beheads the innocent soldiers of an evil man, when he could have let them go, is no hero.'

Gripped with outrage, Fitzwarren slammed a hand down against the well's stone wall. 'It's no more than Hood would have done!'

He jumped back as the water in the well spat up at him.

'The well disagrees.' The Lady placed a hand into the water.

A cloud of confusion crossed his face as he staggered against the side of the well, pain causing him to curl his fingers into his palms. 'What have you done? My head… it hurts so much!'

She smiled as she removed her hand from the well. 'Then please, drink from the water…'

He didn't hesitate. Leaning forwards, Fitzwarren plunged both of his hands into the well, cupping them together, using them to scoop water to his lips.

For a few seconds, he sighed with relief as the headache that had so quickly crippled him, cleared. Breaking into a smile, he reached down to take one more drink…

The two outlaws hadn't got far along the path to Beeston, before Marion came to an abrupt halt.

'Stop a minute, Will.'

Scarlet frowned. 'But we need to get back.'

'And I need to be able to tell Robin his father is safe from blackmail over the future of the earldom.' She turned to look back the way they'd come. 'Listen for a moment… I'm sure that if we wait…'

An ear-splitting scream ricocheted through the trees and down the path, making the apple blossom tremble.

‘What was that?’ Will spun around to face the way they’d come.

Marion gave a rueful grimace. ‘I suspect that was Fitzwarren getting the answer wrong.’

‘What?’

Marion put a hand out to Will, bringing him to a halt. ‘He lied to the Lady of the Well for his own ends—and worse—he pretended to love her. So, she gave him to the well.’

‘Chilly!’

‘Very.’

‘He deserved it.’

‘Maybe.’ Marion stared along the pathway. ‘Are the water pouches safe in the sack?’

‘As safe as gold in the sheriff’s pocket while we’re on holiday.’

Marion smiled, sure now that the Lady didn’t need any further help, and that the earldom was safe. As the birds above began to sing, a light breeze fluttered the leaves above them as they retraced their steps towards Beeston.

A few steps letter, Will looked down at his boots. ‘Here, I’ve just noticed, my feet didn’t hurt while we were near the well.’

‘The Lady told me the water cures all bodily ills.’

'In that case, I hope there's some left after the others have had what they need.'

'Why?'

'Cos these new boots ain't 'alf rubbing me feet again!'

THE LADY'S CHOICE

by

Jennifer Ash

A sequel to *Fitzwarren's Well*, which takes place a year later

PROLOGUE

Newly fledged spring leaves danced happily, as a gentle breeze nudged the branches in a tucked away corner of Sherwood Forest.

Beeston Wood, a mixture of thickly planted oak and beech trees, and sporadic glades, had, at its heart, an ancient well. It's depth unknown; the circular stone structure had been there for far longer than anyone could remember.

Despite the calmness of the night, however, the water within the well undulated as if it had been disturbed; yet no one was stirring the waters, nor did anyone attempt to lower a bucket into its depths.

Not far from the well, a woman slept.

Sheltered beneath the thatch of a makeshift

cottage, to the right of the glade, the Lady of the Well slept upon a straw mattressed cot.

Restless, her lips moved in muted mutters, her forehead dotted with perspiration. 'Keep away from the well… must keep away… the water is angry. So angry…'

The Lady rolled over, twisting her blankets around her limbs as a figure loomed through the fog of her nightmare. She flinched as she saw his face—his cruel smile, the curl of his lip full of contempt.

'Fitzwarren… *NO*! I will *not* look. I will not. He's gone, he's…'

A male voice, smarmy and sneering called to her through her mind. 'The Lady of the Well grows impatient… but not impatient enough.'

As each word that the memory of Fitzwarren uttered within the Lady's night terror threaded through her troubled mind, the well's water rotated faster, spraying droplets, like tears, into the air.

The Lady clasped her hands over her ears, desperate to ignore the voice she'd hoped to never hear again; the voice of the man who'd broken her heart, torn her confidence in two, and, somehow, turned the well against her.

Her lips moved, sending her defiance into the waking world. 'No… I will *not* listen, I…'

'Rise from your slumber my Lady. *Look* into the well. See how the water stirs. See how hungry it is… hungry for…'

As the pull of his voice grew stronger, the sound of the water grew louder, fiercer. The Lady battled not to move, not to get up, not go towards the well.

She had resolved never to stare into its depths again.

Not ever.

Her eyes remained closed. 'Pain… the well only causes pain. I tried to do good with it… then you came and…'

Again, water splashed up against the well's stone walls, its ferocity making the lady shiver. Fear crept over her prone body as she spoke in her sleep. 'The water… the people, they… they say…' She gulped, 'What if they're right?'

The voice of Fitzwarren rang through her subconscious state, his fury carrying across the small clearing and into the trees, making the slumbering woman tremble. 'The people say that *you* killed me! The Lady murders… the Lady is cursed… the Lady brings destruction… *The Lady of the Well* kills the crops!'

The Lady groaned in her sleep. 'They accuse *me*. My people say I bring them bad luck.' Her voice cracked with anger, 'But it was you. *YOU* promised me forever, Fitzwarren! *You* said you loved me! You said…'

A howl of laughter came from the depths of her subconscious. 'You claim *I* was the evil one! Yet it was *you* who ended the line of Edgar of Huntingdon! My father and I could have helped rule England! Guided King John's arm. We could have…'

'You deserved your end! The water knew—it *knew*! It saw your dishonest soul and consumed it!' The Lady's body abruptly stilled, along with her anger. She could hear something else—or maybe she just sensed it.

Another voice… a kinder one.

A smile came to the sleeping woman's lips as, peaceful now, she spoke the words of welcome she recited whenever someone came to her for help. 'You have travelled the path to the realm of the Well. What do you want of me?'

The answer came, as if from far away. The voice was soft, humble, beseeching. 'I am here to beg your kindness.'

The Lady of the Well awoke with a start. Clasping her blanket to her chest, she listened, expecting to hear the violent movement of the well's water. Instead, she heard nothing but a gentle ripple.

Surprised, her voice uncertain, her confidence forever shaken after her encounter with Fitzwarren, the Lady spoke to the new voice. 'The water… the water recognises *your* pain…'

Casting her bedcovers aside, she clambered to her feet. As she rose, the well switched its temperament once again. Waves formed across its surface, making so much noise it was if the water was howling in distress. The Lady frowned.

Are my senses cheating me, or did I really recognise another voice? A voice that's welcome and real—not like his *voice—he has gone. He must be gone. It was just a nightmare—a recurring nightmare.*

'I swear I felt loneliness… Whoever approaches feels unwanted… unheeded…'

The Lady of the Well wiped the perspiration from her forehead.

Did my nightmare trick me into imagining nicer things? Is this my mind trying to protect me, or did I really hear her?

'Marion of Sherwood.'

CHAPTER ONE

Marion placed her feet with precise care, avoiding every raised tree root and every fallen twig. Her progress through Sherwood was swift.

'You'd think it was our fault.' Alert, life as an outlaw making her ready to encounter potential trouble at every turn, her words were little more than a murmur on the dawn air. '*My* fault! The way Robin talks, it's as if *I* arranged for last year's harvest to fail all by myself.'

She irritably hooked the bag she carried higher up her shoulder. 'We aren't responsible for the people of Sherwood not having enough to eat.'

Marion hesitated before deciding to take a left turn through a dense thicket of woodland. 'It's only right that we give the villagers all the food we can, but until this year's crops grow…'

A pheasant darted out in front of her, briefly interrupting her conversation with herself.

'I'm just so tired of the bickering. John says one thing, Will says another. Tuck tries to keep the peace between them and falls out with one or the other or both. Nasir is saying even less than usual and poor Much…' she brushed a stray hair from her forehead, 'he's stuck in the middle, trying to be nice to everyone and…'

Marion stopped dead and listened.

'What's that? Hello?'

Straining to hear any sound that should not be there, all she could pick up was the rustle of leaves and the tuneful song of the birds above her.

Trusting her instincts, sure that there was someone, or something, watching her, Marion snapped, 'Herne, if that is *you* keeping an eye on me, then perhaps you'd like to tell your son that I *only* kept some food back for us, so we had the strength to fight for the villagers if we needed to. *Not* because I intended to eat it all myself!'

Fuming at the memory of the assumption Robin had made, she was about to change direction, when a familiar figure appeared from between the thickly placed trunks.

'It's not 'Erne, Marion. It's me.'

'Much! What are you doing here?'

'Following you. You said...' Much looked down at his feet, '...you said you wouldn't leave us again. You aren't leaving—are you?'

'I'm just going for a walk.' Marion blew out a ragged breath. 'What are you doing here, Much? I thought Robin put you on guard duty.'

'Yeah, he did, but I saw you leaving.'

Suddenly weary, Marion said, 'You should be guarding the camp, not me.'

'But...'

Marion came to an abrupt halt, wondering how she could make him understand. 'I just needed some time to be quiet, that's all.'

A smile came to her young friend's face. 'Oh, that's alright. I don't make much noise. Where are we going?'

Turning her face away, Marion started walking again. 'Oh, Much...'

An hour later, as the sun rose higher in the sky, announcing the middle of the day, Marion gestured ahead, along an ever thinning trackway. 'The southern edge of Sherwood already! If only I could walk so fast when I wasn't angry.'

Much cast her a reproached look as he muttered, 'I wish you'd tell me why you're cross and where we're going.'

Stopping, resting her back against the trunk of an oak tree, Marion tried to ignore the aching rumble in her stomach as it reminded her how hungry she was. 'I don't know where I'm going. I hadn't planned to go anywhere. I needed to get away for a while. To think… to…'

Her words faltered and she grabbed the dagger at her belt. Much, equally aware of the unnatural change to the air, drew his sword, as they both tensed, ready to disappear into the forest if they needed to.

They relaxed a second later as a mystical figure appeared from nowhere.

'Herne! You *have* been following me.' Marion replaced her blade.

Much's hushed utterance of, 'Herne!' echoed Marion's as he too re-sheathed his weapon, and waited for the Lord of the Forest to speak.

'Marion of Sherwood. You feel alone.'

Surprised, Marion confessed, 'I… yes.'

Feeling awkward in the background, a rather put out Much mumbled, 'But I'm here.'

Herne's eyes, twinkling in the early morning light, despite being hidden in the shadow of the stag's headdress he wore, focused on Marion. 'The Hooded Man needs you. They *all* need you.'

Much nodded frantically in agreement. 'Yeah! We do!'

'They need food, not me. I am *tired*, Herne. Tired of the arguments. Tired of not being able to help everyone. *Tired* of feeling useless. I need…'

Her words trailed off as Herne raised a hand and pointed forwards. 'You need to follow the path. The path your life has been leading you along since a leaf blew into Nottingham Castle and spoke of a May morning.'

Marion took a sharp intake of breath. '*You are like a May morning…* He said that. Robin said… he said…'

Herne lowered his arms. 'You followed him. You followed Loxley. The choice was yours. It is *still* yours to make every day. You choose to live as an outlaw.'

Marion closed her eyes. 'A dangerous way to live.'

'*What other way is there?'* Herne's reply felt as if

had not come from his lips—but from a memory—from far away.

Marion gasped. 'Robert. Robert said that… the King had been trying to… and…'

Interrupting her once more, Herne rested an ancient, gnarled, hand on her shoulder and told her what she already knew—what she'd always known. 'Herne's Son needed Marion of Sherwood that day. He will *always* need her.'

Acknowledging the truth of what she heard, Marion took a step backwards, before sitting at the base of the oak's trunk.

'He's right, Marion. Robin does need you—they both did.' Much dropped down next to her. 'I need you.'

Flicking her long red plait over her right shoulder, she peered up at the forest god. 'There is not enough food, and the early spring heat parches the earth. Last year's harvest failed, and the food is all but gone. I fear for this year's harvest before it's fully planted. The people of Sherwood will not survive another poor harvest—many won't even live to see it.'

Herne stretched open his arms, as if to encompass the entire country. 'The people of England are hungry.'

Not bothering to disguise the fatigue that had formed dark circles beneath her eyes, Marion's words sounded as weary as her body. 'We cannot feed them all.'

'But you can help protect them while they are at their weakest.'

Marion sighed. 'The men argue. We go round in circles.'

Herne again gestured to the path along which Marion and Much had been walking. 'You stand at a crossroads, Marion of Leaford. Around you lies Sherwood. Ahead lies the road to London. The path you take is your choice—but remember, once the heart of Sherwood beats within you, it beats forever.'

Wiping a tear from her eye, Marion stuttered, 'I don't know if…'

A haze of mist rose around Herne, and he began to fade into the landscape, his final words hanging on the air. 'In the past lies what is to come.'

Much blinked, making sure Herne was really gone, before he looked at Marion. 'He's said that before too, hasn't he.'

'He has. Honestly, it's as if he can't think of anything new to…' Leaping up, Marion replaced the bag to her shoulder. 'Of course, what's gone before!'

'What do you mean?'

'The last time Will and I came this far south I was searching for the Lady of the Well. Do you remember, Much? I collected some of her well's water to cure you of that curse Fitzwarren had put on us.'

'Lord Edgar's son? Aye, I remember. We almost lost Tuck.'

'You were ill too. You all were. I *had* to leave you then… I had no choice.'

Herne's voice floated through the forest towards them. '*You've always had a choice.*'

'I thought Herne had gone?'

Marion gave a faint smile. 'I don't think Herne is ever far away, Much, not when we need him. Come on.'

Much scrambled to his feet. 'Do you know where we're going then?'

'Not really.' Marion moved forwards again, resigned to having company. 'But maybe we should go to see the Lady. Maybe she'd understand why I…'

A worried Much asked, 'You aren't *really* lonely, are you?'

'Sometimes I am… sometimes…'

'But I'm…'

Laying a hand on Much's arm, Marion cut in, her words kind. 'I know, Much, and I will always be here for you too. But sometimes…' She broke off, not sure how to explain. 'Let's go and find the Lady of the Well. She knows how lonely it is to be…' She swallowed at the memory broke off before hastily adding, 'Fitzwarren conned her heart.'

Breaking her stride, a shadow crossed Marion's face. 'Perhaps Fitzwarren is the past Herne meant?'

'Will said he were dead.'

'He is. Just like his father before him.' Marion shuddered, gripping her bag more tightly as she walked forwards. 'Even now the thought of Lord Edgar of Huntingdon's smile… uggh!'

Much grimaced at the memory of Robin's uncle. 'He almost got us all executed. He was a traitor!'

'He was. The Lady was so unhappy when I last saw her—and that was partly *our* fault. Because Robert left Huntingdon for *us*. If he hadn't, Fitzwarren wouldn't have sought to take the earldom for himself. Nor would he have tried to claim the Lady's power as his own.'

Picking up her pace, Marion pushed away her fatigue and hunger, her purpose now clear—she had to get to the Lady of the Well.

Marion's stomach gurgled in an unladylike fashion. 'I'm hungry.'

'Me too.' Much shrugged helplessly. 'I'm sorry, my water pouch is empty. I didn't even bring water—not that there's much left at the camp to bring. I didn't know we'd be going so far.'

'It's alright.' Keeping moving, Marion loosened the ties on her bag and slid a hand inside. 'I have some bread we can eat now, but it'll never last until we get to Beeston.'

Breaking a tiny portion of bread in two, Marion passed half to Much before eating her own while shaking her water pouch.

'I've not got much water left either. At least the Lady of the Well will be able to give us something to drink. I bet her well hasn't dried up like so many others.'

As they resumed their walk, a troubled Much kept vigilant as they passed along a particularly overshadowed stretch of forest track. 'I… umm… I told the others I was going to follow you.'

'You did?'

'Yeah.' Much felt awkward as he confessed. 'Will said not to bother. That you'd be back when you'd calmed down. That it's what all women is like.'

Marion's eyes narrowed. 'Did he now?'

‘Yeah.’ Much scuffed at the forest floor with his boot; a worried pink tinge coming to his cheeks. ‘But I said that it was *you*, not “any woman”, and that I was worried.’

Patting her friend on the shoulder, Marion spoke through pursed lips. ‘I think I might be having a little chat with Will Scarlet in the near future.’

‘I know Robin was worried about you, but he went all proud in front of the others.’ Much grunted. ‘That’s just stupid earl’s son stuff if you ask me.’

‘That’s a very good way of putting it.’

Much began to march. Frustration at his fellow outlaws not caring where Marion had gone making him even crosser, now that he’d found her walking to the far side of Sherwood and—worse—heading into potential danger.

‘Robin said he’d look for you tomorrow if you ain’t back. Said he had a good idea where you’d gone—not that he’d tell us where he meant. That was something that sparked another argument between Will and John.’ Much abruptly stopped walking. ‘Where *did* he think you’d gone, Marion?’

Hoping Much didn’t notice her slight hesitation, Marion said, ‘I don’t know.’

‘Oh.’ Much mumbled as he moved forward again. ‘I bet they’s laughing at me. I can ’ear Scarlet right now—"Much is so stupid. How can he look for someone when he don't know where they is?"'

'That's two things I need to talk to Scarlet about when I get back.'

'You are coming back then?'

Marion gave a heavy sigh in lieu of an answer. 'Come on, let me introduce you to the Lady of the Well.'

'Alright.' Much walked a few steps in silence before saying, 'Marion?'

'Yes, Much?'

'Did Robin… Loxley, I mean… Did he really say you were like a May morning?'

'Yes, Much. He did.' A wave of sadness came over Marion as she thought back to that life-changing day when an escaped prisoner had taken refuge in her bed chamber. A day which had led to a life she'd never seen coming; never even imagined.

'They can be quite drizzly, can't they.'

Marion laughed, smiling at her friend. 'I'm so glad you're here, Much.'

'Are you? That's good then.'

CHAPTER TWO

The two outlaws had walked in silence for some time, each trapped in their own thoughts, the little energy they had left going into keeping moving forwards.

Marion glanced at Much from out of the corner of her eye. She knew it was his absolute faith in her, his belief that she knew what she was doing, that kept him there.

He always trusts me and the others—always—well, I hope he's right to trust me this time. I don't even know why I'm so sure that finding the Lady of the Well is the right thing to do. But somehow, I know I must go to her.

Exhaling sharply, Marion thought of the others back at the camp. She pictured Friar Tuck, who she knew would be worried about his 'Little Flower'; she thought of Little John, who would be comparing her behaviour to Meg's, considering it perfectly normal for her and Robin to argue; of Nasir, who—as ever—would be keeping his thoughts firmly to himself. *As for Will…* Marion found her hand going to the handle of her dagger as she thought about her most belligerent friend. *You and I are going to have words when I get back, Scarlet…* The thought almost made her stop walking. Until that moment, despite what she'd implied to Much, she hadn't been sure if she would go back—she hadn't allowed herself to be anything but angry.

But then Much found me and Herne came, and…

An image of Robert of Huntingdon—Robin—filled her mind. She could see him now, sat near the camp fire, his back proud and straight as he leant against the ancient oak tree under which the two of them slept. His hood would be down, his blonde hair shining in the firelight. *He's probably cleaning his knife or polishing Albion. He's never truly still—especially if he's worried or cross.* She was sure they'd be a slight curl to his lips as he worked and a furrow of concentration on his face—they'd be no smile, just the look of pure determination a man gets when he is destined for a purpose he is unable to walk away from. A purpose that required sacrifice. The ultimate sacrifice.

Sometimes I think he forgets that I understand—that I've always understood. That we share the same sacrifice. That I gave up riches and comfort too. That I see what comes for us, that we can't avoid it…

A lump came to Marion's throat as she glanced at Much. She was glad he was always too wrapped in his own thoughts to notice her disquiet.

Sometimes I wish I didn't love Robin—that I didn't love and care for them all… Marion massaged her forehead. She knew it was no good thinking that way. *Herne's right, once Sherwood's heart beats in you, it has you forever.*

Much glanced from left to right. Always vigilant, he felt an extra weight of responsibility as he accompanied his friend through a less familiar part of the forest.

This isn't like Marion. She doesn't just disappear. I must look after her.

Much watched her as she twirled her plait between her fingers, her preoccupied expression doing nothing to ease his concerns. *I wish the others were here.* He peered into the trees to the left, half hoping to see his friends heading towards them.

Why didn't Robin stop her leaving?

Midday had come and gone, and now, as the afternoon light became shrouded in cloud, robbing the land of the earlier sunshine, Marion pointed ahead. 'The road to Beeston. Thank goodness!'

'My feet ache almost as much as my stomach.' Much grumbled, as Marion led them along the road which would take them straight to Beeston's marketplace.

Feeling for a purse within the folds of her cloak, she extracted a few precious coins. 'Perhaps the market will have some food we can share with the Lady?'

'I 'ope so.' Much checked to make sure the way was clear, before emerging from the cover of the forest.

Following on Much's heels, Marion waved a hand to the left. 'The market's that way.'

The hum of gossip from the people moving between the stalls reached them before they saw the rows of tables displaying fabrics, pots, baskets, and more for sale—but precious little to eat.

Much growled far more quietly than his empty stomach did. 'They're selling everything but food.'

After a moment's despondency, Marion dashed forward. 'Apples!'

'What? Where?' Much wove through the market after Marion.

'Over there. Look. I'll get some.' Moving fast, Marion kept her eyes fixed on the dwindling pile of apples at a busy stall ahead of them. 'You have a hunt around the rest of the market. See if there's any other food we can buy for you to take home.'

'Right.' Much darted off in the opposite direction. He decided he didn't want to think about the fact Marion had said, 'for *you* to take home', and not, 'for *us* to take home.'

'Five apples, please.'

Marion was almost giddy with relief at seeing something to eat.

The stall holder, however, had other ideas. 'You can buy two. I don't have many left.'

'Of course. They are not both for me.' Memories of the outlaws insinuation that she had kept back food for herself knotted in her stomach as she passed over a coin.

The stall holder appeared unconvinced. 'It's generous of you to share; food is so scarce. I only have this last sack of apples left.'

Hurriedly putting the two apples in her bag, aware that, should she be attacked on her return to the forest, it was more likely to be for her food than the pennies she carried, Marion muttered a subdued 'Thank you.'

Running a hand through his tousled hair, the apple seller studied her with blatant curiosity. 'We don't often see strangers in Beeston. You are new here?'

'I'm on my way to visit a friend.'

'Well, take care, and, if your journey is to takes you that way, avoid the main path through the forest if you can.'

Marion's chin lifted as she asked, 'Really? Why?'

Passing his next customer a single apple in exchange for a hard-earned penny, the stall holder's expression darkened. 'An evil woman lives there.

They do say it's her fault that there's no food—that *she* caused the poor harvest.'

'How could that be?'

Waiting until his other customer had gone, the man leant closer to Marion. 'She controls the water. Some say she's responsible for the dry streams. The harvest was bad… and now the water is running out.'

Marion felt her heart thud faster. 'Controls the water?'

The grizzled man dusted his palms across his grubby apron as he said, 'Sounds impossible, but I swear she has powers. And we know she's already killed a man.'

'Killed a man?'

'Yes, she…'

'Thank you for your concern.' Marion interrupted with as soothing a smile as she could muster. 'I'll bid you good day.'

I was right to come. I was meant to be here now, at this time.

Holding tightly to the handle of her bag, Marion hurried away to find Much. 'The Lady… I knew something was wrong… I knew it!'

CHAPTER THREE

The Lady tensed. Stood beside the well, she held onto its round stone wall, pleading with the water to calm itself.

In the past—before *he* had come—she'd been able to soothe it with her words if it had become unsettled, whispering kindnesses until the slosh of the water had reverted to its usual serene state. But since Fitzwarren had been consumed by the well's depths, her control had gone, and now, try as she might, the water did as it pleased.

Perhaps if I looked down—addressed the water directly… but I daren't. I daren't!

Now, the sound of two sets of feet, pounding fast, heading in her direction, brought a fresh sense of unease tripping through her. A sensation that was instantly mirrored by the water which, as if listening, formed inquisitive ripples across its surface.

Suddenly, two men appeared from the forest, running fast towards the well.

The Lady spun around. 'Who are you? How did you get down my path? I didn't summon you to my realm.'

'Summon us?' The taller of the men snorted. 'So, you *own* the path now, do you? I bet the sheriff would laugh at that!'

Before the Lady could respond, he threw some water pouches to his companion. 'Is there water in there, Mark?'

Watching as the newcomers approached the water, the Lady felt the now familiar sense of fear flow through her. A crease formed on her forehead. 'Why didn't the path warn me? Normally I know—normally I can feel visitors and ask them their purpose, and...'

Taking no notice of the Lady, Mark looked into the well. 'Yeah. You were right, Roger, we're dying of thirst, and she's got plenty to drink right here.'

Coming to herself, the Lady looked accusingly at her uninvited guests. 'Dying of thirst? What do you mean? I knew the people were hungry, but...'

Roger spat as he spun around to face her. 'You

witch! Don't pretend! You know there's barely any food or water left, because *you* did this to us!'

'No! I swear I…'

Pulling a knife from his belt, Roger waved it towards the frightened woman. 'I'd stop those lies if I were you, or I'll cut your tongue out!'

'No, please, I haven't done anything!'

Roger rushed forwards, holding a blade to her throat. 'Yeah? Then 'ow come your well is full of water, when the river's all but dry?'

She stuttered, the presence of the knife focusing her concentration. 'This… this is the realm of the well…' The Lady licked her lips, before managing to stammer. 'I don't know why the path didn't tell me you were coming… I… You are supposed to ask for help and then I grant…'

'You what?' Mark lowered the first empty pouch into the well to fill with water.

'No! Don't take it!' Forgetting the knife for a split second, the Lady went to lunge forwards, but finding herself trapped, she pleaded, 'The well won't like it!'

Lifting the pouch back from the well, Mark hesitated, uncertain. He'd heard a great deal about the Lady of the Well. He'd imagined a witch—someone cold and unfeeling… not a pale, frightened woman who looked as exhausted as they were. His friend, however, had no such doubts.

'You 'ear that Mark? The *well* won't like it!' Roger gave a scornful chuckle. 'We know all about you, Lady! How many have you cursed? How many have you killed?'

'None. No one!' Backing away, the Lady looked fearfully, not at the men, but towards the well. 'I will try to help you, but the well… it has stopped listening to me. You must answer a riddle—prove your worth—and then…'

'We ain't got time for no riddles, Lady!' Roger pressed the blade closer to her pale neck. 'Our families are weak. They'll be deaths next! There's our worth!'

Mark warily lowered the pouch back towards the water as hunger made his insides contract. 'I bet you've got food too, ain't you?'

The Lady squealed as Roger angled the knife so she could feel its danger bite her flesh. 'Please! Don't cut me! I don't have any food. I haven't done anything to your water.'

As if it had heard her claim, the water in the well started to swirl, causing a whirlpool.

Mark jumped back in alarm. 'What the hell!' As soon as he moved away, the water stilled, so he reached forwards again, but each time he pushed the pouch towards the surface, the water spun in the opposite direction.

'The water... it won't go in the pouch. It's moving.'

'Of course it's moving, it's water. Water flows!' Roger tutted with impatience, keeping his gaze firmly on the cowering woman before him.

'Not in a well, it don't!' Mark failed to keep the panic from his voice.

'Hurry up and fill them so we can get out of here.'

A lifetime of experience warned Mark that it was never worth annoying his often impatient friend. Telling himself he must be imagining things; he pushed the pouch back into the water.

Once again the water leapt out of the way.

'It won't go in. The water's dodging the pouch.'

Roger snapped, 'Don't be ridiculous.'

'I'm telling you that it won't...' Mark's words were cut short as the well sprayed a wave of water over the side of its stone wall with an accompanying crack of anger. A noise that was followed by something much much worse...

'Ahhh!' Dropping the pouch, a soaking wet Mark backed away in alarm, his eyes wide with fear. 'A hand! There was a hand it...' Scrambling away from the well, he stared at the Lady. 'What magic is this?'

Roger threw the Lady to the ground, demanding, 'What's happening?'

As the callous, hungry, thirsty man loomed over her, a knife in his hand, the Lady stuttered, 'You must listen…'

'I saw a hand.' Mark wrapped his arms around himself, the thin veneer of bravado he'd tried to show completely gone as he whimpered, 'A hand. There was a hand! It tried to grab me!'

Roger was about to dismiss his friend's claim, but one look at Mark's white face and he changed his mind, bellowing, 'WHAT HAVE YOU DONE TO THE WATER!'

'Nothing! I did nothing! I tried to warn you…'

Dropping the other empty pouch to the floor, Mark grabbed his friend by the elbow. 'Let's go, Roger! Please! Leave her.'

Throwing his prisoner to the ground, Roger continued to wave his knife towards the Lady. 'We need water, you wicked hag!'

'I would have let you—I would have… but it doesn't listen to me anymore.'

'You just want it all for yourself!' Roger shook his head in disbelief, but nonetheless, he sheathed his weapon. 'We'll be back. With others!'

CHAPTER FOUR

Joining Much on the far side of the market, Marion wasn't surprised to discover he'd had no luck in finding additional food.

'There's nothing else left to eat, apart from a few old onions that not even Tuck would think of eating.'

'We need to hurry, Much.' Feeling a sense of urgency that she couldn't have explained to anyone beyond her outlaw friends, Marion patted her bag. 'I've got two apples. There are others, but the stall holder is only allowing two per person.'

Looking back towards the apple stall, Much asked, 'I could buy two more for the journey home.'

'Good idea. Here.' Marion fished some more

coins from her pouch. 'I must go on. The apple seller said something about the Lady—the people who live here, they think she's a murderer.'

Much's eyes widened. 'She ain't, is she?'

'No, Much. But something is wrong.'

'Then I should come with you.'

'We need food, Much. I'll be fine. The Lady is my friend.' Marion pointed to a gap between two beech trees on the other side of the market 'See that path into the forest?'

'Yeah.'

'Once you've got the apples—if there are any left—then just follow it. It leads to the well.'

'Right.'

'Oh, and don't worry if you feel as if you're drowning as you go. That's normal.'

Much's eyes widened even further. 'What?'

Hurrying away, Marion called over her shoulder. 'Don't worry—I'll explain later.'

Retracing his steps, Much made a beeline for the apple seller's stall.

'Could I buy two apples, please?'

'No.'

Much was taken aback. 'But, you have apples! I have money to pay for them.'

'Two per customer.'

'Yeah.' Much was confused. 'I want two.'

The apple seller rolled his eyes. 'You must think I'm stupid. I saw you with your pretty lady. She got apples for both of you.'

Hunger and fatigue had frayed Much's usually infinite patience. 'Marion ain't my lady, she's Robin's lady. She's my *friend*.'

Unmoved, the stall holder folded his arms across his chest. 'Makes no difference. You can have one of 'er apples.'

'But them apples were for someone else. This two will be for us.' He tapped two of the apples on the table. 'One for me and one for Marion.'

'Are you deaf?'

Anxious to catch up with Marion, Much glanced towards the forest. 'I *need* those apples. I'll pay you double.'

The man was unimpressed. 'What use is your money when there's no food to spend it on!'

'Well, what can I buy some apples with then?'

Suddenly, Much had the apple seller's full attention. 'Umm… how good are you at sewing?'

Much wasn't sure he'd heard correctly. 'Sewing? But… but Marion needs me, and…'

'That's the price. You sew up the breeches I ripped yesterday, and I'll pay you with two apples.'

'I'm in a hurry.' A sheen of perspiration broke out on the back of Much's neck. *I have to get to Marion!*

'You'd best be on your way then.'

Much's eyes narrowed. 'Ten apples and I'll sew your breeches.'

'Ten! That's robbery.'

'Seven then. Seven apples. One for each of my friends.' He gulped, hoping that the meagre sewing skills he'd developed over the years in the forest, while attempting to keep his own clothing in one piece, were up to the job.

'I could have sworn this was the path to the well, but maybe I'm wrong.' Marion examined the area around her. 'Will and I found it easily last time.' She started to walk again, paying more attention every single tree as she went. 'There was… yes, apple blossom. This is it.'

Concerned by how many brambles and how much bracken had been allowed to grow across the path, Marion drew her dagger. 'Why is it so overgrown?' She cut her way through a particularly stubborn bramble branch. 'When Will and I were here, the path to the Lady of the Well was clear—apart from that swine Fitzwarren, of course.'

Progressing stealthily onwards, she saw the way ahead was more open. 'Looks like someone *has* cleared it ahead. It's only narrow but…' Marion stopped and listened. '…others have been here. *Recently.*' She looked around her, spotting a track that led to the right. 'They must have joined the path from there.'

Moving with more care, Marion sighed. 'Nasir would be able to tell me how many people have been here. If only…'

The resonance of Herne's voice filled her mind. '*Beware the hand at the well.*'

A shiver of cold made her pause. 'The hand? Whose hand? The Lady's hand?'

Herne urged, '*Hurry.*'

Much stabbed the needle through the tough material of the stall holder's breeches. 'This ain't just a rip! Half the leg is off!'

Listening to the brisk trade of the last few apples being sold, Much called out, 'You'd better not sell all them apples before I'm finished!'

'You'd best be sewing faster then, hadn't you!'

'This needle's blunt.' Much groaned and he muttered to himself, 'Stay safe, Marion. I'll be there soon… Ouch!' He sucked his pricked finger. 'Well, soon-ish.'

The faint trickle of running water met Marion's ears as she cautiously made her way along the path.

'I don't remember a stream nearby.'

With a growing sense that something was wrong, she listened intently to the flow of the water. As she got nearer, it no longer sounded like a stream running, but as if trapped water was lapping—lapping angrily—against stone.

'That's not a stream, it's the well!' Holding her dagger out before her, she crept forwards. 'I was right. Something is wrong here… Last time I found the path, the Lady called me into the realm of the well—I was dragged towards her as if I was drowning in its water, but now… it's as if…'

Marion clamped her lips closed and backed into the undergrowth as she sensed, one second before she heard them, two sets of running footsteps heading in her direction.

CHAPTER FIVE

'Come on!'

'I'm running as fast as I can.' Mark was almost breathless as he pounded along the narrow track. 'It's alright for you! You aren't soaking wet!'

Lacking sympathy, Roger grunted, 'You'll dry.'

Keeping as close to his friend as possible, constantly peering around, as if waiting for something, or someone, to leap out at them, Mark blurted, 'How did she do that to the water? She didn't even touch it. I swear it roared at me. And that hand…'

'It was just a trick. There was no hand.' Roger swerved to the right, running off the track, so that they were crashing through the trees, on a more direct route back to Beeston.

'I'm telling you…'

Not wanting to admit how unnerved he'd been by the thought of what Mark claimed to have seen, or confess to having felt frightened while they were by the well, Roger sniffed dismissively. 'Must have been doing something magical with 'er mind or something. Making you see stuff that wasn't there.'

'We didn't even get any water!'

'Not this time. But we're going back. With the others. If all the men from the town…'

Mark shook his head. 'They'll never come, not when they hear what…'

Abruptly stopping, Roger spun round, holding a palm up to his companion, who almost careered into him. 'Shush!'

'What is it?'

'Someone's watching us.'

'No one's here.' Sweat broke out on Mark's forehead. 'Are you saying that the forest is watching us?'

Roger was about to tell Mark not to be so ridiculous, but the words stuck in his throat. Drawing his knife, he called out, 'Who is it? Who's there?'

As they stood, back to back; waiting, listening, it dawned on both men that all they could hear was the persistent flow of rushing water. No leaves stirred. No birds sang.

'What has she done to us? To the forest?' Mark whimpered, 'Can you hear water?'

Roger hadn't wanted to admit how wrong things had felt while they'd been near the well, but now the change to the atmosphere, combined with his normally brave and sensible friend's pasty complexion, sent a frisson of fear down his back. Yet, pride stiffened his resolve as he stubbornly denied the evidence of his own senses. 'You're imagining it!'

'I tell you; I can hear water!'

'I can't.' Grabbing hold of Mark's elbow and towing him along. Roger kept his eyes forward, ignoring the sweat that had broken out on his forehead. 'I can hear something though… someone is definitely…' Diving between the trees, Roger seized Marion's arm, preventing her from using her dagger as he yanked her from her hiding space. '… watching us.'

'Get off me!' Frantically trying to free her assailant's hold, Marion yelled again, 'Get off!'

His fear forgotten, Roger looked Marion up and down, as if she were a prized possession. 'What have we here?'

'I said, let go of me!'

Roger swiped the knife from Marion's hand, 'A woman lurking in the trees with a weapon! What sort of hellish place has this forest become?'

Moving swiftly, Marion kicked Roger on his left shin.

'Ouch!'

'If you don't let go of my arm, you'll find out just how hellish this place can get!'

Increasing his grip on Marion, Roger gestured for Mark to help him hold her as he growled, 'You're with *her*, aren't you?'

Before Marion could answer, Mark cried out, 'I can still hear it!' Not attempting to hide his fear, he swung round so that he was facing their prisoner. 'You *can* hear it too—can't you?'

Increasingly worried for his friend, Roger demanded, 'What have you done to Mark!'

'Nothing!'

Roger had had enough. Pushing Mark away, he stood behind Marion, wrapping an arm around her neck. 'Why were you hiding in the forest?'

'I heard you coming—I thought you might try and steal my food. I have so little left.'

Unconvinced, Roger pressed, 'Are you saying you aren't with *her*?'

Unable to struggle now, the unwashed scent of the two men assaulted her nostrils. Marion forced herself to stay calm. 'Who is *her*?'

Mark licked his lips nervously. 'The Lady of the Well. She… she's mad!'

Her concern for the Lady growing, Marion choked out, 'What do you mean?'

A thought that had been nagging Mark managed to break through his fear. 'Look at 'er Roger, she's a lady too. She talks too good for a villager.'

Mark backed away, leaving Roger to hold their prisoner alone. 'Who *are* you?'

'I'm Marion of Leaford.'

'Leaford? Never 'eard of it.' Roger held her tighter, causing Marion to tilt her chin upwards a fraction, so she wasn't strangled.

Wrapping his arms around himself, Mark's gaze darted anxiously left and right. 'You *are* with 'er, aren't you!?'

'No! I'm here to help her!'

'Help *her*!' Roger couldn't believe what he was hearing. 'No one helps her! She's a killer.'

A frisson of fear waved over Marion. 'Killer?'

'A man went into the forest and never came out.' Roger kept his arm in place, but relaxed his hold a fraction. 'It has to have been her.'

'She's killed no one.' Marion yelled, 'Now let me go!'

Twisting free from a surprised Roger's grasp, Marion ran towards the roar of the water.

'Grab her bag! She's got food.'

Marion heard Roger calling out behind her. She kept going, but hunger had robbed her of her usual speed, and she'd only been running for half a minute, before Mark had caught up with her.

His hands reached for her bag, trying to yank it from her shoulder.

'Let go!'

As Marion fought against Mark, Roger cut the bag's strap from her shoulder.

'Got it!'

Cursing under her breath, Marion knew it was pointless to try and get it back, so she continued to flee towards the water. As she ran, she could hear Roger shouting to his friend.

'Come on, Mark!'

'The water… The well. I said, I can still hear it!'

'Come *on*!'

Only when she was sure that the men had gone, did Marion risk looking over her shoulder.

Where are you, Much?

CHAPTER SIX

Caring nothing for the mud that clung to her once beautiful gown, the Lady dropped to her knees and, steeling herself, peeped over the stone wall and into the well's water, for the first time in a very long time.

Helpless, as the water swirled faster and faster, creating angry whirlpools which spun in ever decreasing circles, she pleaded with its murky depths. 'I tried to stop them! They're desperate—they act out of fear.'

The direction of the water changed abruptly, sloshing violently.

She tried again. 'I told you. I do not trust myself to use your magic. Not since…'

Breaking off, she suddenly felt the weight of the past year crash through her. Jumping to her feet, a burst of passion shot from the Lady's lips. 'Fitzwarren tainted *everything*. It was *his* hand that Mark saw—*his hand*. Wasn't it?'

The water stopped moving, as if it was listening to her.

'*Wasn't it*!' The Lady's heart pounded as, bunching her palms into fists, she repeated, 'His soul has seized your power and I've had enough! Your water does good. It *did* good. I helped you to help others. Can't you remember?!' She stared again into the well, its once clear water an ever-changing mix of green and black. 'How can I break Fitzwarren's control?'

She shuddered as bubbles gathered on the water's surface. Slowly at first, they formed and popped, formed and popped… more and more of them, faster and faster.

Half afraid and half determined, the Lady demanded, 'I said, how can I break his…?'

'You cannot.' The voice of Fitzwarren erupted with the bubbles on the surface of the water, each of which resounded with his harsh, mocking laugh.

Holding onto the wall, doing her best not to let her legs give way, the Lady whispered, 'I will find a way.'

'You will not—for now you are the one they call evil.'

She drew in a sharp breath, but the well took no notice, as the voice of the man who'd ruined her life rose up from the water. And this time, it wasn't a dream.

'I named myself for Fulk Fitzwarren—who, like me, was robbed of his birthright by another nobleman. Fulk Fitzwarren fought for what was his. He was a hero!'

The Lady's knuckles whitened as she gripped the well's wall. 'A hero who beheads the innocent soldiers of an evil man, when he could have let them go! Huh! Fulk was no hero.'

Fitzwarren screamed through the bubbles. 'It's no more than Robin Hood would have done!'

'NO! This is the past—the *past*—stop it! We've had this conversation!' A wave of water leapt from the well, soaking her from head to toe. 'You are *my* well—I am *yours*.' Shouting now, the Lady proclaimed across the clearing. 'How long are you going to torture me with the echo of his words?'

The answer she received, instantly robbed her of her thinly mustered confidence.

'These are not echoes…' Fitzwarren's voice rang out. 'With each day, since the well took me, I've grown stronger. The power of the water is mine now.'

The Lady let go of the wall so fast, it was as if she'd been burnt. Backing away from the well, she felt a sob rising in her throat.

'No… no…'

Her eyes filled with hopeless tears, as Fitzwarren's trapped laughter rose from the well and rebounded throughout the clearing.

CHAPTER SEVEN

Tired, thirsty, and worrying about what had happened to Much, Marion finally stepped into the Lady's glade home.

Marion's fears were immediately confirmed as she saw the Lady of Well, crouched next to her charge. Rushing forwards, Marion knelt next to her friend, as the well's water lapped dejectedly within its confines.

'My Lady, it's Marion—Marion of Sherwood. I came before, do you remember? A year ago, when…'

The Lady brushed her matted blonde hair away from her face as she looked up in wonder. '*You* called me. The well told me you were coming. Its thoughts have been silent for so long—but somehow your approach broke through… it could feel your pain, and despite everything, it wanted to tell me.'

'*My* pain? I'm alright, just hungry that's all. And thirsty. I don't suppose…' Marion approached the well, but was soon consumed by disappointment. 'Oh. I hoped your well would be spared the drought. I thought I heard it lap, but there's no water.'

'There's plenty of water in the well. Just now, I saw…' Puzzled, the Lady rose to her feet and stole herself to peer back over the round stone wall. 'It's gone. The well must be protecting itself. Hiding its water. Others came; they tried to take some water without asking.'

Marion frowned. 'Two men? One with a knife?'

'Yes. How did you know?'

'We met. They stole my food.' Marion massaged her throat. 'I'd brought apples to share with you, but now… I'm sorry, my gift to give you is gone.'

'You are kind. No other would consider my need for food.' The Lady looked down, as if noticing just how wet and muddy her once beautiful gown was for the first time. She smeared her dirty palms down her front. 'After you came last time, other people visited for a while. I tried to help them—sometimes I could, but soon… the water… it wouldn't listen to me.'

'What went wrong?'

'It didn't take long before Fitzwarren was missed by his own kind. Men-at-arms came to search for him. They didn't find him, of course—but they did find rumour. Soon, it was declared that he must have met his end in the forest.'

Marion understood the situation all too well. 'Let me guess, rumour became gossip, and the gossip led directly to you—the only person who lives within the heart of Beeston Wood. A lone woman with magic at her disposal.'

A single tear escaped from the Lady's eyes, trailing a hesitant line through the grime that coated her face. 'The people of Beeston are convinced I killed him, but it was the well—the well took him. And now...' She diverted her gaze from the well with a shudder and made her way to her tumble-down home, '...now it won't let me forget. *He* won't let me forget.'

As the Lady sank down onto what had once been a solid doorstep, Marion, sat next to her. 'What do you mean?'

'Fitzwarren comes to me in dreams—taunting me. Telling me I am responsible for his death. I no longer...' She broke off, trailing into silence.

'My Lady?'

The Lady seized a stone and threw it angrily at the well's wall. Seething, she screamed across the clearing. 'All those men wanted was water. But you wouldn't let them take what they needed!'

Her shoulders shaking, the Lady breathed out slowly and turned to Marion. 'I warned them. The men that came. Maybe if they'd asked me if they could have some water before they tried to take some… but, no—even then it would have been no good. I can't control the well anymore. And the well… it…'

'The well? What did it do?'

'It cursed them.'

CHAPTER EIGHT

Much threw the sewn-up breeches at the stall holder will ill grace. 'Here. Now, give me my seven apples.'

Holding up the repaired clothing with a critical expression on his face, the stall holder tutted. 'This work isn't worth more than four!'

Much's temper was close to breaking. and his fingers were sore and spotted with pin pricks of blood. 'You promised seven!'

'Yeah, well, you never said you were so bad with a needle!'

Gritting his teeth, Much repeated, 'You *promised* seven!'

The stall holder shrugged, 'Life's tough!'

'You think your life is tough! You want it to

get tougher?' Much drew his dagger, wiping the grin from his companion's face. 'Now, give me the apples!'

The afternoon light was beginning to fade, and clouds gathered above the canopy of the forest as Marion and the Lady sat, huddled together beneath the trees.

'You say your friend Much came with you?'

'He was worried. He followed me. He'll be here soon.' *He should have been here ages ago.*

'Your other friends will be missing you.'

'Maybe.'

Some of her old astuteness returning, the Lady shuffled around to face Marion. 'You feel guilty at having left Sherwood.'

'I wasn't helping anymore.' Picking a twig up off the floor, Marion scored its end through the earth beside her. 'I couldn't stand the bickering. The men are so difficult when they're hungry. Without me there is one less mouth to feed.'

'Yet you feel their absence keenly.'

'Yes.'

'The last time you came here, you did so to save them all. This time you come to escape.'

'I suppose I felt alone. Something told me you'd understand.'

'That I do.' The Lady let out a loaded sigh. 'Maybe that's why…'

'Why what?'

'As I said, the well hasn't told me anything since the villagers began to say I'd killed Fitzwarren… but *you* broke through. The well told me you were coming. That you were lonely. I wonder why it could reach me to tell me that, when Fitzwarren has managed to block me from it at all other times?'

Shifting awkwardly, Marion gulped against her dry throat, her stomach aching from lack of food. Silence coated the clearing as both women became lost in their own thoughts. It was only when the well went quiet, it's water now as calm as a millpond, that Marion spoke again.

'You truly haven't asked anything of the well since the rumours started?'

'I kept asking for a while, but nothing I requested was granted. After a while, I gave up.'

As the Lady spoke, the water in the well stirred again, cautiously, as if it was eavesdropping on the women's conversation.

'The more the rumours against me took hold, the more difficult it got to control the well. The water started to act differently—it fought against my bidding. In the end I became afraid, Marion.'

'Afraid? Afraid of the well?'

'More of making another mistake? What if someone else dies because of me? I was such a fool.' The Lady clambered to her feet and glared at the well's round stone wall. 'If I hadn't fallen for Fitzwarren in the first place, then the well wouldn't have taken him.' She faltered, fear etched on her face. 'I… I think his soul is trapped in the water—he's made it… cruel. I… I've heard him… and seen…'

As the Lady's words petered out, Marion returned to the well. The water surged as if angry. 'Your emotions are tied to the well. Perhaps the water is responding to you.'

The little colour left in the Lady's face drained away. 'So it *is* my fault.'

'I didn't mean that.' Licking her lips, working moisture into her dry mouth, Marion added, 'I think you're underestimating the damage love can cause when cruelly offered. Could the well be feeling your sadness at being alone and your fear of being hurt again?' Marion laid a gentle hand on her friend's arm. 'It responded to your emotions before, remember?'

'How could I forget?'

Feeling light-headed from lack of food, Marion coughed to try and clear her dry throat. 'I must have some water soon. Do you think...? Could you ask the well?'

'What if it curses you?'

Marion was thoughtful. 'I don't think it will—not if you give it permission to quench my thirst.'

'I don't know.'

Although she understood the Lady's anxiety, nonetheless Marion persisted, 'Please, or I'll have no strength to return.'

'So, you *are* going to return to Sherwood?'

'I'll have to take Much back. But whether I'll stay after I've done that... I don't know yet.'

As the Lady reluctantly returned to the well's side, Marion ventured, 'If I did go back, you could come too. Live with us in Sherwood, or find a new home in one of the villages.'

'I am tied to the well. I've tried to leave before...' She risked a glimpse into the water, which immediately splashed at her, as if spitting in her direction. '...but the well will not release me. As you can see, it is so angry.'

'I know how it feels!' Marion stared at the now raging water. 'If Robin and the others didn't take me for granted, then maybe I wouldn't feel neglected. Last on the list!' She blew out a tight breath, surprised at what she was saying, but unable to stop. 'Neglected! I feel that... That's it! I understand now!' Marion watched as the water sloped over the well's sides once again. 'The water *does* feel what you feel. You have been keeping away from the well because you were afraid of doing wrong—but, in the process, you have neglected it, and it doesn't like it.'

The Lady focused her blue eyes on Marion, not sure if she trusted herself enough to believe what her friend was saying.

Sensing the Lady's unease, Marion went on. 'You could be right about the water being tainted by Fitzwarren's soul—but it is the well, not the water, which holds the magic. The well *has* got a soul—a soul that's twinned with yours.'

Feeling her legs weaken from lack of food, a long walk, and little water, Marion rested heavily on the side of the well.

'Twinned souls...'

Marion's head started to thump, a persistent ache forming on her forehead. 'Please, please ask the well for water. I trust you. It will be alright.'

'It's been so long since I...'

Trying not to beg, knowing the Lady wasn't delaying because she was cruel, but because she was afraid of hurting her, Marion was running out of ideas, when she remembered how her requests had been granted on her previous visit to Beeston.

'A riddle maybe? Last time I had to answer a riddle to receive help from the well.'

Biting her lip, the Lady muttered, 'This place does not favour you, Marion of Sherwood. You were ill last time you came and now you are faint with hunger and lack of water.' She took a deep breath, 'I'll try to get you water, but remember, there should be no sickness or bodily weakness in this realm—and yet you *are* weak. So am I… My magic has broken and so the path is open to anyone. I cannot promise that…'

'*Please* try. I won't blame you if it doesn't work.'

'Alright.' With a small dip of agreement, the Lady rested against the well. 'But forgive me if I fail, Lady Marion.'

CHAPTER NINE

'Marion, where are you?'

Much shouldered his way along the overgrown path. He could see where someone had been there before him. Hoping he was following in Marion's wake and no one else's, he moved as fast as he could. 'Robin will kill me if anything happens to her!'

Moving too fast, Much tripped, falling to the ground with a thump. Flushed with embarrassment, knowing he'd never have got his foot caught in a tree root if he'd had enough to eat, Much quickly jumped back up. 'Robin won't have to kill me—at this rate, hunger will get me first.'

The Lady's whole body quivered in time to the lap of the water within the well. Taking comfort from Marion's presence, she stared into the water as she spoke. 'You have travelled the path to the realm of the well, what would you ask of me?'

'I would like a drink please. A drink so I have the strength to walk back to Sherwood.'

Marion hadn't finished speaking before the contents of the well began to seethe, sending rivulets cascading down the stone sides.

The Lady spoke quickly. 'Marion of Sherwood, I challenge you to a question and a riddle. If you accept the challenge and correctly answer the question, you will be allowed to drink from the well and have enough strength to walk home. Do you accept the challenge?'

'I do.'

'Your question. What will happen if you do not return to Sherwood?'

Surprised by the question, Marion felt herself sway slightly, and her head thud with dehydration. 'I… I don't know. Perhaps nothing. Perhaps the others will manage, but…'

The water hissed, causing a fearful shadow to cross the Lady's face. 'That is not the truth of your heart, Lady Marion.'

'I know.' Marion rested against the well's wall as she admitted, 'If I do not return, Robin will suffer. I will suffer. My friends will miss me. Sherwood will suffer.'

The Lady's voice rang with relief. 'An honest answer. Now you will answer the riddle. Tell me, Lady Marion…'

The water suddenly screamed, forcing the Lady and Marion to reel backwards, their hands over their ears.

'No!' The Lady doubled over, as if in pain.

'My Lady?' Marion lowered her hands, and reached out to her friend, only to freeze as a familiar voice erupted from the well's depths.

'Do you bring me company, my Lady?'

'*Fitzwarren*? It can't be.' Marion leapt in front of the Lady, protecting her as a hand punched its way through the surface of the water.

'No!' Horrified, Marion saw the large, gnarled hand shoot forward. Its skin was that way after so long in the water. A split-second later, a sodden, tunic-covered arm drove the hand forward. It shot towards the women, seizing Marion by the elbow.

'Let her go! Let her go!' The Lady pleaded as Marion fought against the disembodied hand and arm.

Fitzwarren's voice gurgled, his tone almost silky, as he mused, 'Let go of the woman who bought about my downfall? I don't think so.'

The Lady fell backwards as, with demonic strength, Fitzwarren dragged Marion towards the well.

Kicking out with her legs, her free arm fighting in vain to unhook the curled fingers that held her in a vice-like grip, Marion spoke through panting breaths, 'I can't hold on… Help me! He's trying to throw me in.'

'Finally! Revenge!' Fitzwarren's sub-water chuckle sent fresh bubbles rippling across the water.

'You evil…' The Lady dove forwards, and linked her arms around Marion's waist, attempting to pull her free. 'You did this to the well, Fitzwarren! It wasn't me—it *was* you!'

'You shouldn't have allowed the well to take a mind as strong as mine.' His smug laugh filled the glade. 'Come and join me, Lady Marion. I'm sure you like to swim.'

The Lady's shoulder's strained with the effort of trying to free her friend. 'I command you…'

Fitzwarren let out an angry bellow. 'You command *nothing*! You gave me to the well—and now it's mine!'

As her right foot was lifted from the ground, and her head wrenched closer to the water, Marion cried out, 'Robin!'

Fitzwarren gave a mocking laugh. 'Your outlaws are far away, Lady Marion. You *will* become part of the water.'

'No!' The Lady renewed her efforts to prevent Marion from being taken.

Marion closed her eyes, concentrating all her effort into keeping her left foot firmly earthbound. But she was tired, and despite herself, she could feel her body weakening. Fighting to control her emotions, she tried to focus her mind on the images in her head... the people she had to stay alive for.

Robin was smiling at her. The outlaws were together, laughing as they sat around the camp fire; planning a raid, tending a wounded arm or leg, polishing swords, stringing bows...

Marion's comforting thoughts were cruelly wiped from her head as the clearing was filled with a new, terrifying sound; an almost deafening crescendo of pounding water... and voices. So many voices... screams and begging... so much distress...

Fitzwarren's voice thundered out in triumph, 'Listen! Listen to the turmoil of the well! Hear the souls of those lost to the water.'

'Noooo... please, I beg you...' Letting go of Marion, the Lady clapped her hands to her ears and fell to the ground. 'I command the well. It's mine. I'm the Lady of the Well. Those cries are from before my time here... before me... I'm good, I'm...'

'Utterly helpless... a failure. A murderer in the eyes of the people... and now... I will take Marion of Sherwood.'

Without the Lady to help her, Marion was easily wrenched from the ground. Within seconds her face was dangerously close to the water, her hair soaked by the splash of its sea-like waves. Her scream of terror mixed with the pleas of the helpless petitioners of long past coming from the well's depths.

The reverberation of the water's fury made Beeston Wood's trees shake as Fitzwarren levered his victim ever closer. 'You, my Lady, have condemned another soul to a life in your well!'

'Marion!' The Lady's voice faltered as she saw her friend's exhausted body disappear over the side of the well.

'Robin...' The outlaw's faint plea was lost to the well. Her struggles became weaker and weaker.

'Don't worry, Marion, you won't be lonely. I'll keep you company...' Fitzwarren's laughter rang with confidence, '...for all eternity.'

The Lady sobbed as she ran forwards, helpless to stop Marion's body sinking beneath the water.

CHAPTER TEN

'Marion!'

Much burst into the clearing and ran towards the well in time to see Marion's legs slipping out of sight.

'Who's doing this?!' Confused by what he was seeing, he shouted at the woman he saw. She was freezing cold and soaking wet; her clothing stuck to her skin and water dripping from the hem of her gown.

As Much dashed to the side of the well, the Lady murmured, 'It's him… he's controlling the water.'

As a stunned Much took hold of Marion's ankles, panic lent him strength. 'I'm here, Marion! It's me, Much. I'm here.'

Heaving with all his might, Much was joined by the Lady, but as hard they pulled, the water pulled back, as if Marion was the rope in a tug of war. Every now and then, Marion's face broke the surface of the water and she spluttered for breath, only to be sucked back beneath the swirling well's waters again almost instantly.

Redoubling his efforts, Much frowned. 'How... can... water... be doing this? It looks like...' The thought of what his friends would say, if he had to tell them that he'd been unable to prevent Marion from drowning, lent him more strength as his senses finally allowed him to believe what he was seeing. 'It can't be... it looks like... a hand made from water. *What* is it?'

The youngest of Robin's outlaws trembled with the effort of exertion as the well replied. 'Not what...' A *second* hand broke through the surface and tried to grab Much as well. '...but who!'

Much's stomach flipped as he narrowly avoided being seized and lifted off his feet. 'Marion!'

Fitzwarren's laughter became manic as, giving up on Much, he tightened his hold on Marion.

Shaking water from his hair, Much closed his eyes. *What would Robin do? I wish he was here. I'm... only... Much.*

Much opened his eyes again in time to see the trees freeze into statutes around them. All that moved was the water, him, the Lady, and the strangely disembodied hand that was wrestling them for Marion's life.

Much's shoulder muscles burned as he heard Herne's voice. '*Trust in yourself, Much. You have always been more than the sum of the parts.*'

Much stared in surprise as the water in the well stopped moving.

'*The strength of Sherwood is yours.*'

Privately thanking Herne, Much gave a final, desperate yank, and Marion's body slipped from the well, toppling them both to the ground.

Coughing and spluttering, Marion struggled to breathe. Her hair was plastered to the side of her face, neck and shoulders—but she was alive.

Thank goodness… There was no time for Much to revel in his success however for—to his horror—he saw that Marion had not left the well alone.

'Look out!' Much yelled as the body of Fitzwarren rose from the ground.

The Lady's scream ricocheted around the forest. 'He can't be alive! He can't…'

Water poured off Fitzwarren by the quart as he lunged towards Marion. 'She's mine! She deserves a life in the well…' He spewed up a mouthful of water '…Marion of Sherwood will be the perfect replacement for me in the water!'

Much kicked out at the staggering man before him, noticing that his faded clothing was only just holding his water-worn flesh and bone together. 'I said, let go of her!'

'Oomph!' Fitzwarren let out a squelchy groan as Much kicked him again. 'I'll never let go… she's going to…' Fitzwarren's words caught in his throat, 'to… be…'

Clutching his throat he rasped, 'I can't… breathe… I…'

The Lady ran to Marion's side, tenderly wiping the wet hair away from her eyes.

'Can't… brea…' Fitzwarren's words broke off and his knees bent, forcing him to sink to the forest floor. A moment later, his whole body crumbled, and he fell forwards, landing with the thump of a heavy wet sack.

A potent hush fell, before the Lady of the Well dared to ask, 'Is he… is he gone?'

Not trusting the evidence of his own eyes, Much prodded the body with his boot. 'Who is he?' When the fallen man didn't move, Much amended his question. 'Who *was* he?'

Exhaling, the Lady asked, 'He's *really* dead?'

'Yeah.' Much stared at the bedraggled nobleman's body. 'Ow did he do that? He was breathing in the water, but he's all dead now he's on land?'

A small smile came to the Lady's face as she heard the water in the well trickling happily from side to side. 'His soul became entwined with the water—now he's left it, the spell is broken. It's over. Thank goodness.'

The Lady's smile died on her lips as she rushed to Marion's side. 'Please tell me you're alright.'

Her eyes struggling to focus, Marion coughed again as she looked around her. 'Much?'

'I'm here.' After helping Marion to sit up, Much tapped his many pockets. 'I got apples. One each for you and me, one for the Lady, and some for the others.'

'Well done, Much.' Marion smiled, but her voice was hoarse, and she shivered with cold.

Suddenly self-conscious, Much sat next to her and stared at the ground. 'Herne, he helped me.'

'Of course he did. I told you, he's never far away when we need him.'

'But, I'm just…'

Marion shook her head, spraying tiny beads of water across the glade in the process. 'You are just one of the bravest men I know. And my friend.'

'Oh, ummm… thanks.'

Leaving the two outlaws to gather their breath, the Lady moved to the side of the well. Staring into the now crystal-clear water, she nodded in satisfaction.

'The spell has lifted now he's gone.' She turned back to Marion and Much. 'The water is free. Can you hear it? I can feel it coming back to me.'

With Much's help, Marion rose to her feet. 'I wonder, would the well help us now? I really need a drink, and I'm sure you do, don't you Much?'

'More than a portion of Tuck's stew.'

CHAPTER ELEVEN

'What's she doing?' Much whispered as they watched the Lady speak words of encouragement to the well. 'I thought she was getting us a drink.'

'You'll get your drink.'

Much brushed his hands together, trying to dislodge some of the dirt and dust that coated his palms. 'I really need one after walking all the way here, sewing them 'orrible breeches, and then dragging that body away to hide it in the woods!'

Marion placed a hand on his shoulder. 'It's a magical well, Much. I'll explain properly later, but first… Hang on, sewing *what* breeches?'

Much wrinkled his nose. 'They stank.'

'*Breeches?*' Marion gathered what remained of her plait in both her hands and squeezed out as much water as she could. 'I think you'd better tell me about that later too.'

With Much at her side, Marion moved closer to where the Lady was holding out her arms over the well, as if she were giving it a hug.

'Forgive me, my well. I will never again trust anyone so unworthy.'

The water gave a musical tinkle as if accepting the apology.

Satisfied, the Lady gestured to her friend. 'Now then, Marion of Sherwood, you have already answered the question. That just leaves a riddle to prove your worth to the well.'

'A riddle?' Much looked worried. 'I won't have to answer one as well, will I?'

The Lady gave him a kind smile. 'No, Much. I'm sure the Lady Marion will share her water with you.'

'Good! I ain't no good at riddles.'

Marion stepped forward. 'I'm ready.'

'Very well.' The Lady closed her eyes, the water swaying as she spoke. 'Many arrows remain inactive. Openly neglected…'

Much stared at Marion as a light mist gathered around them. He half expected Herne to appear, as the strange lady continued.

'…The hunter cannot hunt without his aim. Who steadies the hunter's arm? Who ensures his mark is a fair one?'

Marion gave a soft chuckle. 'The water is trying to tell me where I belong, but it's alright. I know. I've always known. Herne was right, it is about choices.'

'Choices?' Much was none the wiser. 'Is that the answer then? Do we get water now?'

'No, Much, the answer is Marion. *I* am the answer.'

As the water trickled in agreement, the Lady smoothed the stones of the well's wall with her hands.

'That is correct. You may fill your water pouches. Please, take whatever you need.'

As Marion unhooked the empty water pouch from her belt, Much confessed, 'I didn't get that riddle. I knew I wouldn't.'

'Don't worry. Come on.' Marion quickly filled the pouch, and took a long drink, gasping as she said, 'I think that's the best water I've ever tasted.'

The Lady felt a weight lift from her as she asked, 'Tell me, Marion of Sherwood, are you still hungry?'

'Hungry… well, yes, I must be. But, no. No, I'm not!'

'There is no weakness in the realm of the well.' The Lady looked down at her gown and smiled as she saw it dry before her eyes. 'Thank goodness. My power has truly returned to me.'

The Lady addressed Much, as Marion refilled her pouch. 'Once Marion has collected some more water, you must drink it too. While you are within this realm, your hunger will fade.'

'Great! 'urry up Marion! I'm starving.' He passed her the pouch he had hanging from his belt. 'Maybe fill this one too, for later.'

The Lady began to chant as she watched her friend fill their pouches. 'The hungry belly speaks foolishness, making the speaker a fool. The thirsty mouth speaks anger, making the speaker bitter. Once there is food, the foolishness is removed from the fool. Once there is drink, the bitterness is taken from the angry.'

Marion couldn't help but laugh. 'You should meet Herne sometime. I have a feeling you'd get on.'

'Yeah, he don't make a lot of sense sometimes neither.' Much reached out an eager hand as Marion passed him a pouch. He gulped the contents down in three huge, thirsty gulps. 'That's better!'

As Much wiped a hand over his mouth, the Lady patted the wall of the well affectionately, before touching both Marion and Much on the shoulder, drying their clothing from head to toe. 'My mind feels so clear. Thank you, Marion. I don't think the spell would have broken if you hadn't come back.'

Marion smiled as the weight and cold of her sodden clothes disappeared. 'You would have found a way, but now I must go. Herne was right—I chose my path many years ago.'

'And Robin needs you.'

'Sometimes I wonder, but…'

The Lady interrupted. 'You love him, and so you'll go.' She paused, before adding, 'I will miss you, but I too have a path to tread—to guide people along.'

Exchanging a hug with Marion, the Lady looked around her, as if seeing her home for the first time in a long time. 'I feel as if a fog has been lifted. I see what I must do. I cannot bring my people food, but I can give them water and take away their hunger pains. Just as you can give your people protection and a guiding hand.'

'You're right. Thank you.' Marion hooked her water pouch back to her belt. 'Come on, Much, it's time we headed back to the camp.'

'I'm glad the well managed to tell me you were coming.'

Marion smiled. 'Despite Fitzwarren blocking your connection to it.'

'It knows you are special, Marion of Sherwood. You helped it before. The well does not forget.' Peering up at the sky, the cloud of the evening gathering above them, the Lady said, 'It gets late, you could stay until tomorrow.'

'Thank you, but we'll camp down for the night on the way.'

Sad that her friend was leaving, but knowing she was right to do so, the Lady looked back into the well. 'Can I ask a favour of you, Lady Marion? Will you deliver a message on your way home?'

Much nudged Marion as they crossed from the forest into Beeston market. 'Is that them?'

He gestured to the two men sat on some upturned barrels on the edge of the market, chatting quietly as townsfolk came and went around them.

'Yes. That's them.'

'Did they really steal from you?' Much kept his eyes on the men as they approached.

'Just the apples. They were hungry, and that one... Mark, I think his name is... I think Fitzwarren got the water to do something to him… it certainly scared him.'

The outlaws were only a couple of paces away when Roger spotted them.

Getting to his feet, Roger backed away, his voice shaky. 'We can't give you the apples back. The children ate 'em!'

'Good.' Marion gave them a contented smile. 'I'm glad they found a good home.'

Surprise flashed in Roger's eyes. 'You are?'

'I have a message. From the Lady of the Well.'

Mark backed away from Marion even faster than Roger had done. 'I don't want it! We don't want anything from her—ever. I've only just stopped hearing water!'

'You stopped hearing water because the spell that had stolen the power to control the well from the Lady has been broken.'

Roger spat to the ground. 'So there *was* evil!'

'There was.' Marion tried to reassure them. 'And now it has gone. The Lady bid me tell the people of Beeston that the path to the well is open, and there is water for you all. There's enough to tend your crops and fill your drinking vessels.'

Roger's forehead creased with confusion and distrust. 'But we… we tried to steal from her.'

'All is forgiven.' Marion smiled.

Much muttered under his breath. 'But don't ever steel nuffin again!'

Keeping her eyes on Roger, Marion explained, 'Once you have travelled along the path of the well, you'll need to answer a simple question and a riddle, then the realm of the well will welcome you.'

Much added, 'You could clear the path of branches and stuff for the Lady on your way. That would be helpful. And show her you'se sorry.'

Mark's gaze travelled from Marion, to Much, on to Roger, and then back again. 'No more raging water? No more hands in the well?'

'I pulled the hand out.' Much spoke with grim satisfaction. 'It's gone.'

Roger's surprise that such a young man had battled something magical, was clear. '*You* did?'

'Yeah. *I* did.'

Marion patted Much's back. 'Come on, let's go home.' She turned to face the path that ultimately led to the outlaw camp. 'It's up to them now.'

As they headed towards the road north, the outlaws could hear the townsfolk gathering around Roger and Mark behind them. Much was worried, 'I hope the Lady's magic don't wear off to fast, so we don't start feeling hungry 'til we get back.' He muttered.

Marion agreed. 'And I hope that Tuck's got some food to cook with when we get there.'

'Me too. At least we can take them an apple each, though. They'll like that, won't they.'

'They will.'

EPILOGUE

As they reached a more familiar part of Sherwood, Much led the way through a thicket of closely planted oaks.

'Marion?'

'What is it?'

'You won't go away *again*, will you?'

Looking at her friend's troubled face, Marion shook her head. 'No, Much, I've chosen my path. I've made my choice.'

She put a reassuring hand on Much's arm.

And they continued on to camp.

Marion had felt Herne's arrival before she saw him—a faint figure in the distance, beckoning them home.

'The lady returns to the forest. The hunter will take his aim, and the mark will be met.'

You may also enjoy…

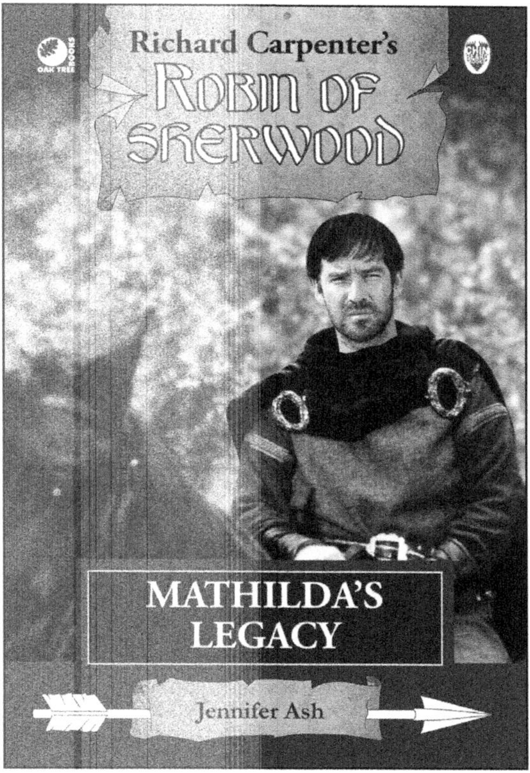

You may also enjoy…

Natsumi Ito
—presents

Tu es ma détective chérie

MY DEAR DETECTIVE

MITSUKO'S CASE FILES

3

CONTENTS

CASE 11
His Brother's Keeper (Part 3)
No.21
No.12
!
MR. HIROSE!
CREAK
GOOD MORNING.
MAY WE HAVE A MOMENT OF YOUR TIME?

...
THIS IS LOVELY!
WOW!
COMING ON STRONG ...
MIGHT IT BE IMPORTED? MY GOODNESS...
YOU MAY NOT. I'M BUSY AT THE--
...
I HEARD THAT YOU ACCOMPANIED HITOYA TO ENGLAND.
HOW DID YOU TRAVEL? BY TRAIN?
FIRST CLASS, I'D IMAGINE.
...
THERE IS NOTHING I CAN TELL YOU.
OH, NO NEED TO BE SO CAUTIOUS!

I'D LOVE TO TRAVEL EUROPE BY TRAIN.
A PLEASANT LUNCH IN THE DINING CAR...
DOESN'T THAT SOUND GREAT?
MUH-ME?!
OH.
WELL...
MAYBE I'D RATHER EAT SOMETHING HOMEMADE, LOOKING OUT THE WINDOW...
OH MY!
THE YOSHIDA FAMILY LIKE TO MINGLE WITH THE MASSES?
MASTER HITOYA WENT...
REPRESENTING THE YOSHIDA NAME.

WHERE ELSE WOULD THE MASTER BE, IF NOT IN FIRST CLASS?
DO NOT CONFUSE HIS TRAVELS WITH SOME LEISURELY *HOLIDAY.*
WAS HE IN FIRST CLASS WHEN THE TRAIN DERAILED?
BUT OF COURSE!
OH?
THAT'S STRANGE.
THAT FIRST-CLASS CAR...
WAS WHOLLY CHARTERED BY THE FOREIGN MINISTER.
FOREIGN MINIS
INVOLVED, RETURNS
IT SAID SO IN THE PAPER.
MR. HIROSE.
WAS HITOYA REALLY ON THAT TRAIN?

...
IT'S NONE OF YOUR CONCERN.
THEN AT LEAST TELL ME.
I KNOW...
THAT YOU DON'T THINK MUCH OF ME.
BUT I AM A SON OF THE YOSHIDA FAMILY...
PLEASE TRUST ME, JUST THIS ONCE.

WHY IS MY BROTHER LYING TO ME?
キイ
CREAK
...
SO THE JIG IS UP, HUH...

CLAK...
I SHOULD'VE KNOWN YOU'D FIGURE IT OUT.
HITOYA...
I'M SORRY I LIED TO YOU.
SAKU...
I'LL TELL YOU EVERYTHING.

LET ME START FROM THE BEGINNING.
EVER SINCE I WAS LITTLE...
THIS AUTUMN
WEAR A SHAWL
FEATURED GOODS
I'VE BEEN ENAMORED WITH THE CATALOGUES FROM THE DEPARTMENT STORE.
KA-CHAK
ガチャ
Master Hitoya.
SKRITCH SKRATCH SKRITCH SKRATCH
Your father has something important to--
Master Hitoya ...?
SNIP SNIP
じょきじょき

GORGEOUS GARMENTS FROM ABROAD.
OSTENTATIOUS ORNAMENTATION.
I WATCHED, AND I LEARNED.
Finished!
What is it?
NOTHING CAPTURED MY IMAGINATION MORE.
...
A little brother?
That's right!
He'll be here next week.
Be nice to him.
GAWP

If I may...
Sir has not told him till now.
A...
Haven't I?
AND THAT...
little brother?!
WAS WHEN I MET YOU.
What a strange creature.
Is it going to be okay...?
IS HE A PUPPY OR SOME-THING?
WHIMPER
WHIIINE
I DIDN'T KNOW HOW TO ACT.

AFTER ALL, I'D NEVER HAD A LITTLE BROTHER BEFORE.
SWFFF
BOO!
YEAAAARGH!
SAKU ?!
I CAN'T COUNT THE TIMES I MADE YOU CRY.
Er... That was to ward off evil!
IT'S A VENE-TIAN MASK!
YEAH!
Don't be scared.
Really?
SEE? IT'S A KITTY!
NOR THE TIMES I TRICKED YOU.
Blow!
PHBT

What is a little brother, anyway?
Someone who's small and gullible...
Someone who cries all the time...
Someone I find myself caring about.
What're you doing?
Do you like drawing?
No, I--
Do you wanna be a painter?

DOFF
I just like clothes!
Wow!
Wow!
This is my collection!
You could be a clothes-making person!
...
Yeah.

Now that you mention it...
maybe I could.
ONCE IT'D BEEN SAID OUT LOUD...
MY IMAGINA-TION RAN WILD.
FIRST, I'D STUDY ABROAD.
Maybe someone will have me as an apprentice...
I'll have to learn while traveling.
I want to see the world for myself!
I WAS YOUNG AND BLIND.

BLIND...
TO THE TRADITIONS THAT SHACKLED MY FAMILY.
They're in a fix now that the wife is gone...
What do you mean?
Well, there's Saku.
Yoshida Shimako
She left behind a son!
He's not related to anyone.
Maybe they'll give him away?
I LOOKED AT MY BROTHER, WHO--UNLIKE ME--DIDN'T HAVE ANCESTRY ON HIS SIDE...
AND I WONDERED.

WHO WAS THERE FOR HIM NOW?
How did I fail to notice?
Of course.
That's the eldest son's job.
I'm sorry...
my dear little brother.

I BURNED ALL MY SKETCHES.
I WAS ASHAMED I'D BEEN SUCH A DREAMER.
I DIDN'T REGRET DOING THAT.
I tell you, Hitoya's really grown up!
I had no clue what was going on in his mind till just recently.
But now, he wants to know about the business!

Maybe I could send him to a meeting in my place.
What's that you're reading?
Just learning about work, is all.
Wazzat?
The company policy.
THIS TIME, YOU QUICKLY OVERTOOK ME.
BUT SOME-THING WAS DIFFERENT.
You should teach me, too!
LIKE ALWAYS, YOU WANTED TO FOLLOW IN MY FOOTSTEPS.

IT FIT YOU LIKE A GLOVE!
YOU WERE BRIGHT.
AMBI-TIOUS.
NOT TO MENTION, OUTGOING.
People believe in him!
WEAR A SHAWL
What if he were to inherit the company?
...
What just popped into my head?

BUT I TOOK THAT NIGGLING FEELING...
AND I STOWED IT AWAY.
THEN WHEN I WENT ABROAD...
IT WASN'T FOR MY OWN SAKE.
IT WAS FOR THE FAMILY.
FOR MY LITTLE BROTHER.
FOR THE GREATER--
Sorry to keep you waiting, Monsieur.

Well, well!
You like my designs?
Very much!
BEAM
Especially this low-waist one.
Look at the cut of the skirt...
How do you come up with these things?!
I'd love to bring this back to Japan!
So you like fashion, *mon bébé*?

I love it!
My name is Elisa Hubert.
Would you join me for tea?
GASP!
Ah, er...
Um...
Look at you.
"BÉBÉ" ?!
THAT EMBER I'D ONCE STOWED AWAY...
You're like a little newborn.
EH?!

QUICKLY FLARED UP INTO A GREAT BIG FIRE.
This is so strange!
I've never had this much fun before.
Hitoya?
I have something for you.

It's a ticket to Paris.
2938
NOT TRANSFERABLE
Victoria to
DOVER
1st Class
The train leaves in two days.
Huh?!
If you wish to study under me...
However ...
settle what you need to settle first.
I do not know what it is that burdens you...
but before you make a choice...
find your own words.
Then speak.

Dialogue is a virtue, *mon bébé.*
You're finally starting to grow up.
CLAK
パターン…
CREAK…

Master Hitoya!
What are you doing, out late every night?
There are only two days till your meeting.
I've been meeting with Elisa Hubert.
...?
The designer?
Yeah.
She's been showing me how she works.
What in tarna-tion?
What is the--
Can you believe it?
Showing *me!*

She gave me a ticket to Paris.
I've always wanted to be a part of that world.
Since I was little!
This might be my chance!
Hwuh--
Hold your horses.
Let's calm down.
Do you mean to say...
that you would leave everything to your brother?

And what of everyone's expectations of you?
GASP!
!
Master Hitoya!
It's all so heavy.
Shouldering Saku's burdens.
And the family's.
I know better than anyone that I'm not cut out for it.
I hate that I'm so selfish.
And despite everything...

I have to be a good brother to him.
I'll go back home.
As soon as I can.
Once I'm home...
this fire in me will once again peter out.

Master Hitoya...
Are you certain about this?
Yeah. Let's go.
...
SHRIEK!
Master Hitoya.
...?!
CHATTER
CHATTER
CHATTER
A train has derailed!
On the other track!
Look! It's going up in flames!

You can claim that you were in this accident.
This is your chance!
Perhaps you lost your memory!
This may be an opportunity to escape the family.
After all, you are an accomplished liar, no?

I DRAGGED HIROSE INTO THIS.
IT'S NOT HIS FAULT.
SAKU...
I WANTED TO TELL YOU.
BUT I WAS AFRAID.
IF YOU THOUGHT LESS OF ME...
I COULDN'T LIVE WITH--
OH *MAN!*
SO YOU DON'T HATE ME!
THAT'S A LOAD OFF.

YOU'VE GOT DREAMS! THAT'S GREAT!
BETTER HURRY BACK TO ELISA AND RETURN THAT WATCH, HUH?
I'VE NEVER THOUGHT LESS OF YOU FOR ANYTHING.
AND I NEVER WILL.
REMEMBER WHEN WE FIRST MET?
THAT DAY...
YOU GAVE ME A TEDDY BEAR.
THANK YOU FOR THAT.

EVER SINCE...
YOU'VE BEEN MY FAVORITE BROTHER IN THE WHOLE WORLD.
FORGIVE ME!
THE BLAME LIES WITH ME!

IF ONLY I HADN'T PROPOSED SUCH A TEMERARIOUS SCHEME...
TREMBLE TREMBLE
WAH!
STARTLED
HIROSE!
DON'T CRY!
SO...
WHAT'RE YOU GONNA DO?
RIGHT... FIRST AND FORE-MOST...
I WANT MY BROTHER TO BE HAPPY.
I'LL THINK ABOUT IT ONCE HE'S IN FRANCE.
WOOF?
ARE YOU SERIOUS?!
COME ON!

THIS IS ABOUT THE WHOLE FAMILY!
WHY'S EVERYONE DECIDING THINGS BY THEMSELVES?!
SURE, LET HIM GO TO FRANCE, BUT TRY *TALKING* ABOUT IT FIRST!
SHEESH.
LISTEN... I MIGHT HAVE AN IDEA.
CASE 11 GOES ON

カチャ
KA-CHAK
AN IDEA? WELL, LET'S--
CASE 12
OH!
WHAT ARE YOU ALL GOSSIPING ABOUT IN HERE?

CASE 12
His Brother's Keeper
(Part 4)

PUTTING YOUR HEADS TOGETHER TO HELP HITOYA?
I HAVE A SUGGESTION MYSELF, ACTUALLY.
HOW ABOUT A TRIP TO THE DE-PARTMENT STORE?
THE ROOFTOP AMUSEMENT PARK COULD BE STIMULATING.
HIROSE!
GO FETCH THE CHAUFFEUR.
COME ALONG, HITOYA.
EXCUSE ME.
MISTER--

CLAK
WUH...
WHAT'S THE DEAL, SAKU?!
YOU'RE NOT GONNA CONVINCE MY DAD!
ONCE HE'S MADE UP HIS MIND, HE'S NOT CHANGING IT.
FOR HIM TO UNDER-STAND...
IT'S GONNA TAKE MORE THAN TALK.
DO YOU REMEMBER THE DRESS I WORE AT DINNER YESTERDAY?

YOUR FATHER GAVE ME THAT.
I can't possibly...
A dress this fancy?
I'll probably just spill something on it!
Don't worry about that.
Clothes are made to be worn.
It's a beautiful piece, isn't it?
That's the fruit of somebody's hard work.
AS A SALESMAN ...
HE HAS RESPECT FOR THE MANUFAC-TURERS.

WHAT IF HE WOULD UNDERSTAND?
MAYBE YOU TWO JUST ASSUME HE WOULDN'T.
LET'S BRING SOME OF YOUR BROTHER'S SKETCHES AND GO AFTER THEM.
...
THAT'S YOUR IDEA?
SO WHAT?
WELL, SINCE YOU'RE SO ASSERTIVE ABOUT IT...
I CAN HARDLY SAY NO, CAN I?

ALL RIGHT!
WE GET OUR PICK OF THE LITTER.
HE'S BEEN DRAWING THESE FOR SO LONG!
WOW, THESE ARE SERIOUS.
LOOK, THESE PATTERNS USE A WESTERN LAYOUT!
IS THIS REALLY HITOYA'S ...?
I WONDER WHO TAUGHT HIM...
DID HE LEARN ALL BY HIMSELF?
HMM...
I... THINK SO...

Saku!
We made a new set of clothes for Tyrant!
IT WAS MOM.

THE ROOFTOP AMUSEMENT PARK?
YES.
TO SEE THE NEW SKY TRAM, IS IT...
THANKS, HIROSE!
SAKU, SIR!
I WISH YOU THE BEST OF LUCK!
RIGHT!
THERE YOU GO.
OUR BRAND-NEW CABLE CAR.
BUSTLE
BUSTLE
I BELIEVE I SHOWED YOU THE BLUEPRINTS ONCE.
CHATTER
CHATTER

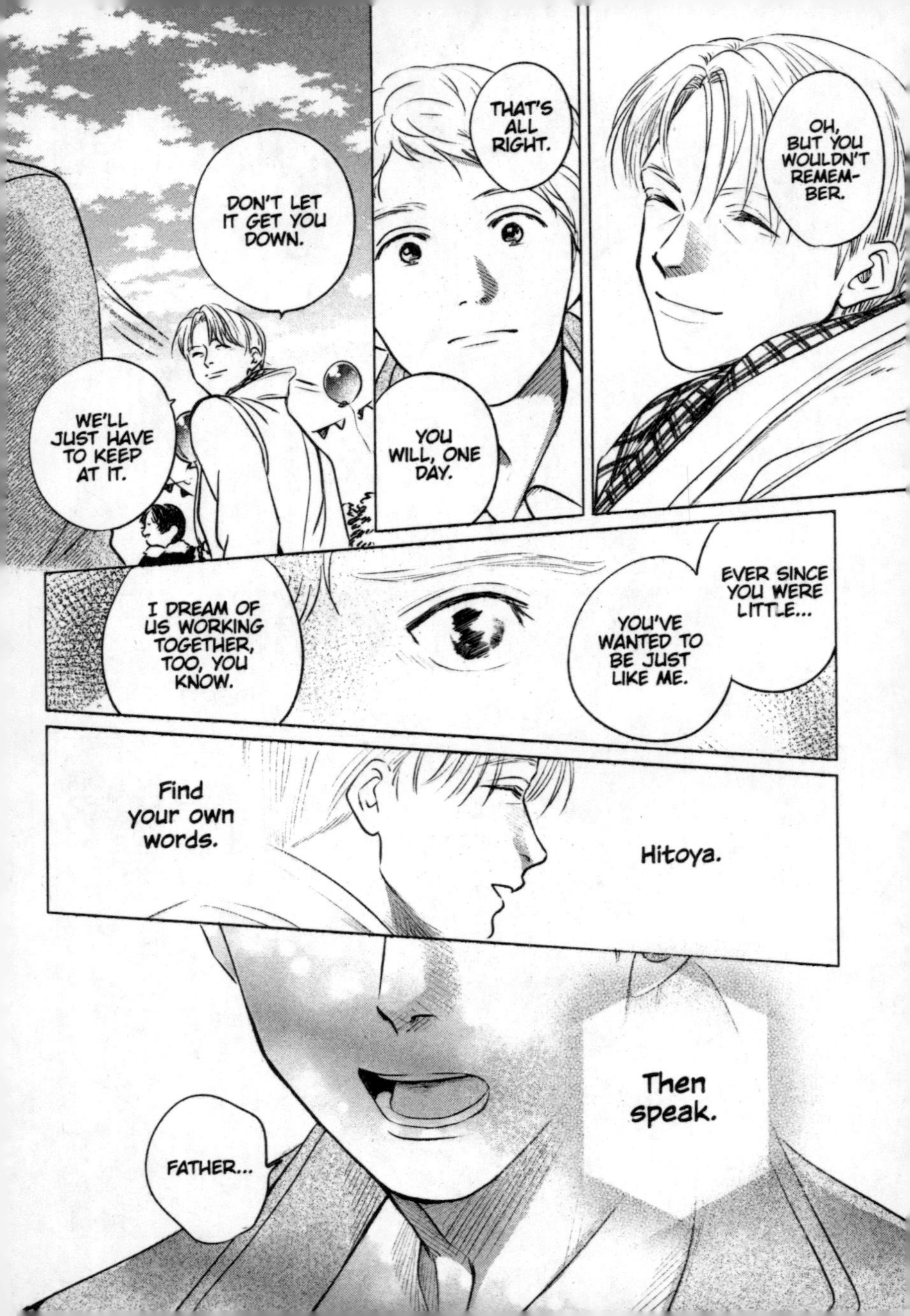
OH, BUT YOU WOULDN'T REMEMBER.
THAT'S ALL RIGHT.
YOU WILL, ONE DAY.
DON'T LET IT GET YOU DOWN.
WE'LL JUST HAVE TO KEEP AT IT.
EVER SINCE YOU WERE LITTLE...
YOU'VE WANTED TO BE JUST LIKE ME.
I DREAM OF US WORKING TOGETHER, TOO, YOU KNOW.
Hitoya.
Find your own words.
Then speak.
FATHER...

WE...
NEED TO TALK.
...
HOLD ON A DARN MOMENT.
WE'RE SUPPOSED TO FIND HIM HERE?!
BUSTLE
WHAT!
HI, LADY.
BUSTLE
HOW'S ABOUT A BIRD'S-EYE VIEW?
AFRAID OF HEIGHTS
SOWWY...
I FORGOT...
WE'RE NOT SO HIGH... I CAN HANDLE IT...
GASP!
GASP!
OH!

...
IT WAS ALL A LIE?
HITOYA...
OF ALL THE THOUGHT-LESS--
WE'VE BEEN WORRIED SICK ABOUT YOU!
WHAT WERE YOU THINKING?!
I CAN'T DO IT.

I'M SCARED.
I CAN'T TELL HIM WHO I REALLY AM.
I'LL ONLY DISAPPOINT HIM.
KLABAM
ガタッ
ガタッ
KLABAM
TUNK
!
WHAT ARE YOU DOING?!
IT WOULD DIVIDE THE FAMILY.
HEY! HITOYA!

WE BROUGHT SOME-THING!
YOUR LIFE'S WORK!
CATCH!

WRONG GUY!
GAH!
...
WHAT'S THIS?

THIS WAS SHIMAKO'S.
A Primer
Renewing Clothes
Vol. 1
...
WHAT ...?
You know, dear...
Hitoya comes to me a lot lately.

I think he might be keen on clothes!
Oh, here it is.
I used this book in my studies way back when.
A Primer
If only boys could go to school for dress-making!
That sure would spell trouble for the business.
Though Hitoya's always wanted to be like his old man.
There you go assuming things again...
What was that?
If you ask me...
being so close to someone ...
makes it easy to lose sight of who they are.
It's all the more important to *talk*.
No matter if you're related by blood...

family doesn't make itself.
It's something we all have to work for.
You designed these in school?
Wow.
Well, well!
You can tell a good design?
Not at all.
But I don't need to know anything about design...
to know that the effort you put in is beautiful.

Oh, darling...
I love that about you.
...
HITOYA.
DID YOU DRAW THESE?
WHEN I WAS LITTLE ...
MOTHER TAUGHT ME.
IT'S BEEN MY DREAM EVER SINCE.

I CAN'T INHERIT THE BUSINESS.
I WANT TO PURSUE THIS.
AND IF POSSIBLE...
I WISH YOU'D SUPPORT ME IN THAT.

HUH?
REALLY?
BUT...
I THOUGHT YOU WANTED TO WORK TOGETHER.
I MAY NOT KNOW MUCH ABOUT DESIGN.
BUT...
HITOYA ...
OF COURSE I WILL.

I CAN SEE YOUR BEAUTIFUL EFFORTS.
BESIDES ...
CLOTHES ARE MADE TO BE WORN.
WE CAN'T LET THESE GO TO WASTE!
I'LL SELL THEM FOR YOU.
THAT WAY, WE BOTH GET WHAT WE WANT, RIGHT?
FATHER...
THAT'S SUCH A GREAT ATTITUDE.
I ADMIRE THAT ABOUT YOU.

SAKU!
DID YOU KNOW ABOUT ALL THIS?
I WOULDN'T SAY I *KNEW*... MORE LIKE...
WE SLEUTHED IT OUT! WE *ARE* DETECTIVES.
HOH HOH HOH!
SAKU!
SEIZE THE MOMENT!
YOU SHOULD TELL FATHER WHAT *YOU* WANT, TOO!
YOU KNOW...
YOU *COULD* INHERIT THE BUSINESS!
YOU CAN'T SAY THAT, FATHER!
THAT'S PUTTING PRESSURE ON HIM ...!
HM? WHY NOT?
AH. RIGHT.

BEAM
WELL, LET'S HEAR IT, SAKU!
I...
HAVEN'T THOUGHT ABOUT IT...
REALLY.
YOU BOTH HAVE THESE GRAND DREAMS.
I WISH I COULD BE LIKE THAT.
I'M JUST...
NOT SO GREAT AT THINKING ABOUT MYSELF.
I LIKE THE DETECTIVE JOB, THOUGH.
YOU COULD SAY I LIKE *WORKING*.
BUT I LIKED THE COMPANY STUDY GROUP, TOO.
I GUESS WHEN IT COMES DOWN TO IT...

I WANT TO HELP PEOPLE.
AS LONG AS I GET TO DO THAT...
I'M HAPPY.
HUH?
BUT, WELL...
COMPANY BOSS AND DETECTIVE COULD BE COOL!
LIKE THE HERO OF A NOVEL!
IT'LL BE ALL RIGHT, SAKU.

SEEING YOU SMILE LIKE THIS...
I CAN TELL THAT YOU'VE FINALLY FOUND A PLACE IN THE WORLD.

MAN, AM I PATHETIC OR WHAT?
I'LL BET YOU THINK SO.
しゅん…
SLUMP
NO, WHY?
YOU WANT TO HELP PEOPLE. I THINK THAT'S SWEET.
NAH...
I'M JUST COPYING SOMEONE ELSE.
YEAH? WHO'S THAT?
WELL...
I'VE GOT THIS REGULAR AT SICILIA.

I'LL OFTEN SEE HER FORCE A SMILE.
DOWN IN THE DUMPS, SOME-TIMES.
SHE'LL BE ALL WORKED UP...
BUT NO MATTER WHAT, BEFORE SHE LEAVES?

HER FACE SAYS, "I'LL BE BACK ON THAT HORSE TOMORROW."

I REALLY LOOK UP TO HER.
...
SHE SOUNDS WONDER-FUL!
ALTHOUGH...
MAYBE A BIT WILD.
YEAH.
CASE 12 CLOSED

SO OVER IT

PAPA LOOOOVES RIDES!

*Thick pancakes filled with sweet azuki bean paste.

CHATTER
ワイ
CHATTER
ワイ
POSTCARDS
ASAKO...? MIE...?
CHATTER
ワイ
CHATTER
ワイ
ザワ
BUSTLE
ザワ
BUSTLE
WHERE'D YOU GO?
DON'T LEAVE ME ALL ON MY OWN!
ROLL
コロ
ROLL
コロ
コロ
ROLL
TONK
MROWWWW
MROWWWW

!
POLISH...
CREAM?
POLISH
HEY! YOU SHOULD STAY OUTTA THE ALLEYS!
UM...
I'M SORRY. I LOST SIGHT OF MY FRIENDS...
NO NEED TO APOLOGIZE.
I'LL HELP YA LOOK.

THERE THEY ARE!
GLAD YOU FOUND 'EM.
LOOK AT THEM...
THEY LOOK LIKE THEY'RE HAVING FUN...
WITHOUT ME.
KSH...
FOR YOU.

NOW WHEN YOU LOOK BACK AT THIS, MAYBE IT WON'T BE ALL BAD.
SHEESH, WHAT A DAY...

IT'S SO LATE...
I NEEDED TO GET A NEW LIGHT-BULB!
PERHAPS STOP BY THE NIGHT MARKET?
GOOD IDEA! I WILL.
I'M COMING, TOO!
TAKE CARE, NOW!
LET'S HAVE SOME FUN!
MAKE IT QUICK. WE HAVE WORK TOMORROW.
ROGER THAT!
FLUTTER
LIKE PEAS AND CARROTS, THOSE TWO.
OH MY!
THIS IS GOR-GEOUS!
LA-DI-DA!
MIMI! THERE'S IMAGAWA-YAKI!

WHUMP
OH, SORRY...
IT'S ALL RIGHT.
MISS TAKAMINE?
WHO?
THE DAUGHTER OF ONE OF OUR REGULARS.
WHAT MIGHT YOU BE--
PLEASE!

DON'T TELL ANYONE I WAS HERE!
I JUST CAME TO FIND SOMEONE!
HE HELPED ME HERE ONCE BEFORE...
BUT I DIDN'T HAVE THE CHANCE TO SAY A WORD OF GRATITUDE.
?
SO YOU SEE...
OHOOOO
I, WELL ...
HER FATHER'S A MEMBER OF THE HOUSE OF PEERS.
IT'D BE HANDY IF SHE OWED US A FAVOR!
VERY CRAFTY...
YOU KNOW...
I HAPPEN TO WORK AT THE GINZA DETECTIVE BUREAU.
REALLY?

MIGHT I BE ABLE TO ENLIST YOUR HELP?
I DON'T HAVE MUCH TIME, YOU SEE!
MY WEDDING IS IN ONLY TWO DAYS' TIME!
HE WAS A GENTLEMAN WHO LOOKED DASHING IN A FLAT CAP.
IN ONE HAND, HE HAD A SUITCASE.
HE WORE THE MOST CURIOUS PERFUME.
AND HE HAD TWO MOLES UNDER ONE EYE!
HIS BLACK SHOES GLISTENED IN THE DARK...
PERHAPS HE'S TRAVELING.

OH, WHO MIGHT HE BE?
...
MIMI...
A FOREIGN PRINCE, PERHAPS? HEE HEE.
YEAH, SAKU, I KNOW...
BUT SHE'S BEEN LOOKING FOR A WHOLE WEEK.
AND WE CAN HARDLY BACK OUT NOW.
MIMI! SHE'S GETTING MARRIED IN TWO DAYS!
LESS "OWED A FAVOR"...
IF THAT GOES IN THE GUTTER, THAT'S A CATASTRO-PHE!
MORE "DESPISED."
OH, I FORGOT TO MENTION! HE GAVE ME FLOWERS!

FREESIAS?
NAW, WE DON'T SELL THOSE HERE.
花市
*Sign: Florist.
HOW'S ABOUT YOU ASK THE FLOWER GIRLS?
I THINK THEY'RE OVER THATAWAY TODAY.
!
THOSE ARE THE ONES!
RUSH
HM?

TEN SEN FOR A BOUQUET, MISS!
IF I MAY...
WERE YOU HERE SELLING FLOWERS A WEEK AGO?
SURE WAS. WHY?
BINGO!
WHAT'S HER DEAL?
WELL... WE'D LIKE TO KNOW ABOUT A CUSTOMER, IF POSSIBLE.
TOO BAD.
FORGETTING THINGS QUICKLY IS MY SPECIALTY! ♪

BUT...
I DON'T THINK YOU'D FORGET THIS MAN.
CURIOUS PERFUME, LUSTROUS SHOES, A SUITCASE...
A FLAT CAP ON HIS HEAD.
TWO MOLES UNDER ONE EYE...
TWO MOLES?
ARE YOU TALKING ABOUT EIKICHI?
I GUESS I *DID* PALM OFF A LEFTOVER BOUQUET ON HIM...
"EIKICHI" ...
LEFT-OVER...?

HE'S NOT A CUSTOMER.
YOU COULD CALL HIM... A *FRIEND*, I SUPPOSE.
GO TO HIJIRIBASHI BRIDGE TOMORROW WHILE THE SUN'S OUT. YOU'LL FIND HIM.
HIJIRI-BASHI BRIDGE.
BLACK SHOES POLISHED TO A SHEEN.
A PECULIAR SCENT.
AND A LARGE SUITCASE...

WHY THERE AND THEN, SPECIFICALLY?
HELLO?
MIMI?
しゅん…
GLOOM...
...
SUCH A WONDERFUL LADY...
MISS SAWAKO...
DO YOU REMEMBER ANYTHING ELSE ABOUT HIM?

DID HE CARRY ANYTHING ELSE?
.....
DID YOU SEE WHAT WAS IN HIS BAG?
LET'S SEE...
OH!
HE DROPPED A CAN OF SOMETHING, I REMEMBER.
POLISH
SOME SORT OF CREAM FROM POLAND...
PERHAPS FOR HIS HAIR?
MODERN MEN HAVE A MIND FOR BEAUTY.
ACK
THAT'S THE KIND OF MAN I IMAGINE HIM TO BE, AT LEAST.

MISS SAWAKO... I, ER...
YOU'RE GETTING MARRIED IN TWO DAYS, RIGHT?
I DON'T KNOW HOW TO SAY THIS.
I'M SURE YOU'RE BUSY. PERHAPS YOU SHOULD POSTPONE THIS...
NO!
I WANT TO GO!
I...
WANT TO MEET THAT GALLANT GENTLEMAN ONCE MORE!
BECAUSE... I'VE NEVER FELT LIKE THIS BEFORE.

THANK YOU FOR YOUR HELP, MISS DETECTIVE.
...
I'LL BE JUST FINE ON MY OWN TOMORROW.
SO, AS TO WHO HE IS...
GOT A HUNCH?
I THINK SO.
WE SHOULD GO THERE TOMORROW, TOO.

THANKS.
THAT'S A GOOD SHINE.

A PLEASURE!
WHAT SHE THOUGHT WAS PERFUME...
WAS THE SCENT OF OIL AND WAX.
AND THE SUITCASE, WELL...
THAT'S FOR HIS TOOLS, NOT FOR TRAVEL.
THAT'S THE REASON FOR HIS WELL-POLISHED SHOES...

HE'S A SHOE SHINER.
SHOE SHINE
I'M AFRAID TO SAY...
HE'S NOT THE PRINCE SHE WAS DREAMING OF.

WHY HULLO THERE, MISS.
LOST YOUR WAY AGAIN?
NOT THIS TIME.
I'VE BEEN LOOKING FOR YOU.
ON THAT DAY...
REMEMBER WHEN YOU HELPED ME?
THAT WAS THE FIRST TIME...
I'VE EVER FELT THE SPARK OF LOVE!

...
HEY, I'M HAPPY TO HEAR IT.
SHOE SHINE 5 SEN
BUT YOU DON'T KNOW MUCH ABOUT ME, DO YA?
NO...
SO, I IMAGINED.
YOU CAME TO MY MIND SO MANY TIMES.
EVERY NIGHT I THOUGHT ABOUT WHAT I'D SAY TO YOU IF WE MET AGAIN...
I NEVER KNEW HOW MUCH FUN IT IS TO BE IN LOVE.
BUT NOW I DO!
BET YOU WERE SURPRISED TO SEE HE'S A SHOESHINE BOY.
NOT AT ALL.
MORE THAN THAT...
I WAS SURPRISED TO SEE WHO *I* WAS.

TOMORROW...
I'LL BE MARRIED.
MY FATHER CHOSE THE GROOM.
THAT'S JUST THE WAY OF THE WORLD, I THOUGHT.
I DON'T HAVE ANY PARTICULAR DESIRE TO WORK...
AND MY FRIENDS AT SCHOOL ARE ALL MARRIED.
I HADN'T THOUGHT MUCH ABOUT MY *OWN* LIFE.
SO NOW I'M FINALLY THINKING ABOUT IT.
I'M THE DAUGHTER OF THE TAKAMINE FAMILY.
I WANT TO HONOR MY LINEAGE.
THAT'S HOW I FEEL.
AND NOT BECAUSE ANYONE TOLD ME TO FEEL THAT WAY.
I CHOSE TO BE WED.
AND I FELL IN LOVE WITH YOU, A STRANGER.

ALL OF THAT IS WHO I AM!
I DON'T DISAPPROVE OF MY PAST CHOICES.
AND I HAVE NO REGRETS.
IT'S ONLY THANKS TO YOU THAT I REALIZED WHO I WANT TO BE.

TOMORROW, I WILL MARRY...
OF MY OWN FREE WILL.
I JUST CAME TO TELL YOU HOW GRATEFUL I AM.
THANK YOU FOR HELPING ME.
AND THANK YOU FOR BEING MY FIRST LOVE.

ALTHOUGH I SUPPOSE I'M PUTTING YOU IN AN UNCOMFORTABLE POSITION, TELLING YOU THIS!
NOT ONE BIT.
I'M GLAD.
WISH WE WOULDA MET EARLIER.
I'LL TREASURE THOSE WORDS.
BOW
FAREWELL. I WISH YOU THE BEST!

SWOOP
WHAT DO YOU KNOW...
SHE'S ONE TOUGH LADY.
WHAT IF THEY *HAD* MET EARLIER?
I WONDER WHAT COULD'VE BEEN.

...
THERE'S NO POINT IN FRETTING OVER IFS AND BUTS.
SAWAKO HAS MADE UP HER MIND.
SHE'S GOING TO FIND HER OWN HAPPINESS.

WELL, THIS IS A SORRY SIGHT.

WHY DIDN'T YOU SAY SOMETHING? ***YOU'RE*** THE ONE WHO HAD HIS HEART STOLEN.
SHOE SHIN
5 SENS
IT'S FINE.
IN THE END...
SHE LEFT WITH A SMILE.

THAT'S A GOOD OUTLOOK.
I LIKE THAT ABOUT YOU.
HEH. THANKS.
CASE 13 CLOSED

WE FINISHED UP BEFORE NOON!
DOESN'T GET BETTER!
IT'S A LOVELY DAY. LET'S WALK HOME!
RUSTLE
HM?
RUSTLE
RUSTLE RUSTLE RUSTLE RUSTLE
...
ISN'T THAT--
WHAT ARE YOU DOING DOWN THERE?
CASE 14

OH, HEY! IT'S SHINDOH'S LACKEY!
LOSE SOMETHING? SHOULDN'T A POLICEMAN BE MORE RIGOROUS?
...
OH, DETECTIVES.
HEH HEH...
YOU'RE ON THE MONEY.
I LOST SOMETHING... EVEN THOUGH I'M POLICE...
I'M SORRY. I'M IN A BIT OF A HURRY.
...
WHY DON'T YOU TELL US WHAT HAPPENED?

CASE 14
The Proof Is in the Pudding

SO?
WHAT'D YOU LOSE?
WELL, ER...
YESTERDAY, MR. SHINDOH HANDED ME THIS ENVELOPE.
Kujoh.
Head to the station and put this on my desk.
AND THEN HE LEFT FOR SOME BUSINESS BACK HOME IN KANSAI.
I LOST IT ON THE WAY TO THE STATION...
AND YOU'VE BEEN DESPERATELY SEARCHING SINCE THEN?
CORRECT.

I DON'T HAVE THE SLIGHTEST CLUE WHERE I LOST IT.
AND MR. SHINDOH'S COMING BACK TODAY...
NO DOUBT IT'S SOME REALLY IMPORTANT DOCUMENTS.
I SWEAR, I...
I...
HA HA HA...
I MIGHT BE BETTER OFF NOT BEING A POLICEMAN.
THAT'S GOING A BIT FAR.
I UNDER-STAND THE SITUATION.
WE'LL LEND YOU A HAND.
ANYTHING MORE YOU CAN TELL US?

I...
I COULDN'T POSSIBLY ASK THAT OF YOU!
NO, NO! NONE OF THAT!
YOU SHOULD ASK FOR HELP WHEN YOU NEED IT!
MIMI'S AS GOOD AS A HUNDRED DETECTIVES!
SO?
WHAT DID YOU DO AFTER YOU TALKED TO SHINDOH?
HMM...
I GOT ON THE TRAIN TO UENO.
GREAT.

TO THE STATION!
DEPARTURES
THIS IS THE ONLY ONE THAT'S BEEN TURNED IN.
HRM...
YEAH, IT'S NOT MINE...
ANYTHING SPECIAL ABOUT THE ENVELOPE?
DO YOU KNOW WHAT'S INSIDE?
I DIDN'T OPEN IT.
AL-THOUGH...
THERE WAS SOMETHING SCRIBBLED ON IT.
READ CAREFULLY! -SHINDOH
IT STRUCK ME THAT IT DIDN'T LOOK LIKE MR. SHINDOH'S HANDWRITING.
JUST AS I WAS PONDERING THAT...

I HEARD A LOUD VOICE FURTHER DOWN IN THE CARRIAGE.
You imbecile!
"Sorry" doesn't cut it!
You can kiss today's lunch goodbye!
My, in front of *people*?
THAT'S ALWAYS UPSETTING TO ME.
MY CHEST TIGHTENS UP...
WHENEVER I HEAR SHOUTING.
BUT I REMEMBER NOW!
I...
I WAS CLUTCHING THE ENVELOPE WHEN THAT HAPPENED!

I COULDN'T STAY ON THE TRAIN AFTER THAT.
TUMP
SO I GOT OFF AND WENT TO THE SHINOBAZU POND.
Mister! Could you get that?
YOU SEE...
I REALLY LIKE UENO PARK.
IT REMINDS ME THAT, HEY...
IT'S FOR THESE PEOPLE THAT I DO WHAT I DO.
AFTER THAT, THEN?
UH...
THEN I GOT IN A CAB.

1911-1945, a domestic national police force that engaged in political suppression.

Um...
I'll get off here ...
Ha!
I ain't going *near* the police station. I'm terrified of that place.
I'm Kujoh. Criminal Investigations, Second Unit.
If you've been wronged by the police...
please, get in contact anytime.
I'll do whatever I... can...
I WAS ABOUT TO GET OUT OF THE CAR, WHEN...
Eyaagh!

AN OLD LADY HAD TRIPPED, RIGHT IN FRONT OF ME.
I HELPED HER UP AND WALKED HER HOME.
ONCE AT THE STATION, I'D FORGOTTEN ALL ABOUT THE EN-VELOPE.
I'M ALWAYS LIKE THAT.
I TRY TO HELP PEOPLE...
AND IT BACKFIRES ON ME.
I JUST END UP MAKING TROUBLE FOR SOMEONE ELSE.
LOOK AT ME.
I'M NOT CUT OUT TO BE A POLICEMAN.
I'LL APOLOGIZE TO MR. SHINDOH AND HAND IN MY LETTER OF RESIGNATION.

TEA!
HOW ABOUT A SPOT OF TEA?
LET'S CALM DOWN A BIT, YEAH?
NEWHALL DINER
WHO ORDERED THE CURRY?
MEEE!
THE PUDDING HERE IS TO DIE FOR.
WHAT HAPPENED TO TEA?
GOING ALL-IN, HUH.
YUM...
HM? THIS IS A BEEF CURRY!
YEAH, IT'S KANSAI-STYLE.
THEY USE BEEF THERE INSTEAD OF PORK.

IT SAYS SO ON THE MENU.
BEST-SELLER!
KANSAI-STYLE BEEF CURRY!
Soup 30 sen
over rice
15 sen
20 sen
key 10 sen
Black tea 10 sen
YOU TWO...
YOU SEEM TO BE A GOOD FIT.
IT'S NOT GOING TOO WELL WITH SHINDOH?
SHINDOH IS... WELL, HE'S THE IDEAL POLICEMAN.
HE'S DECISIVE, AND HE'S DARING.
THE POLAR OPPOSITE OF ME.
I'M TIMID AND INDECISIVE.
WE HAD THIS UNDERCOVER JOB THE OTHER DAY.
I WAS PRACTICALLY DEADWEIGHT.

AFTER-WARD...
SHINDOH TOOK ME HERE, TO THIS DINER.
I FELT LIKE WE HAD TO TALK ABOUT *SOMETHING*, SO I STARTED BABBLING ABOUT PUDDING.
I GUESS I BORED HIM.
HE DIDN'T SAY A WORD.
I DON'T THINK MR. SHINDOH LIKES ME MUCH.
HE WENT TO KANSAI BECAUSE THE OSAKA PREFECTURAL POLICE WANT HIM.
WHAT IF HE LEAVES ME BEHIND?
DON'T SAY THAT.

I DON'T THINK YOU'RE WRONG FOR THE JOB AT ALL.
AFTER TODAY, I KNOW WHAT *I* THINK.
YOU'RE PERCEPTIVE.
YOU'RE *THERE* FOR PEOPLE.
I THINK THOSE ARE TALENTS.
AND MORE THAN ANYTHING...
YOU'RE THE KIND OF POLICE OFFICER *I* WANTED TO BE.

BUT...
A GOOD POLICEMAN WOULDN'T MAKE A MISTA--
DON'T CALL IT JUST YET.
THAT GREEN HANDKER-CHIEF YOU MENTIONED?
THAT MIGHT JUST BE THE KEY.
SINCE CAB COMPANIES ARE POPPING UP LIKE DAISIES...
THERE'S BEEN A MOVE TOWARD CREATING BRANDS.
IF THEY'VE GOT SOME SORT OF DISTINCTION, WE'LL FIND 'EM.

IT'D BE BORING IF EVERYONE WERE THE SAME, DON'T YOU THINK?
AWAMOTO TAXI
HM?
THE COP FROM YESTER-DAY!
FORGOT SOMETHING, YEAH?
WHA--?!
I WAS JUST ABOUT TO BRING IT TO THE STATION.
READ CAREFULLY! -SHINDOH

YA JUST RUSHED OFF.
SILLY ENOUGH TO LEAVE YER JUNK BEHIND.
SHAME NOT EVERYBODY'S LIKE THAT.
I--
YOU SAID YOU WOULDN'T GO NEAR IT...
YOU HELPED THAT OLD LADY, RIGHT?
WE NEED MORE COPS LIKE YOU.
SO! WHAT MAKES THIS ENVELOPE SO IMPORTANT?
LET'S TAKE A PEEK INSIDE!
CLUTCH

ER...
SURE!
FLAP
TAPIOCA PUDDING
DON'T YOU TELL NOBODY!
Top Secret
The secret to perfect pudding
UHHH...
I DON'T THINK THIS IS IT...
HUH?
YOU SAYIN' I MADE A MISTAKE, PUNK?
OH, ER, NO, I...

MR. KUJOH.
THERE'S NO MISTAKE HERE.
WHAT?
WHAT'S MORE, YOU KNOW WHAT THIS IS?
THE SOLLUTION TO ALL YOUR PROBLEMS.
NEWHALL DINER
Secret to perfect pudding
PUDDING

カラーン
JINGLE
カラン
JINGLE
WELCOME, SIR!
ザワザワ
BUSTLE
I'M AFRAID WE HAVE NO AVAIL-ABLE SEATS AT THE MOMENT...
YOU CAN SIT WITH ME.
すんっ
GLARE
?!

WHAT'RE YOU DOIN' HERE, YOU--
OH, JUST SIT DOWN, WOULD YOU?
NO THANKS.
OH? WELL THEN, I SUPPOSE I'LL KEEP THIS.
Top Secret
DON'T YOU TELL NOBODY!
TAPIOCA PUDDING
The secret to perfect pudding
RECIPE
Pour one teacup of tapioca into the milk and bring to a simmer. Stir continuously to melt the tapioca.
Once viscous, stir in one teacup of sugar and remove from heat.
THIS IS YOURS, RIGHT?
DO YOU KNOW...
HOW WORRIED KUJOH HAS BEEN?
HOW--

HE THINKS HE'S NOT CUT OUT FOR THE JOB. THAT HE SHOULD QUIT!
WHAT?
WHADDAYA MEAN?
I THOUGHT SO.
YOU'RE NOT VERY OBSER-VANT OF *FEELINGS*.
LISTEN.
YOU NEED TO TREAT YOUR PEOPLE WITH--
KUJOH? NOT *CUT OUT* FOR IT? THAT'S THE DUMBEST THING I'VE HEARD ALL WEEK.
THE MAN'S THOROUGH. TREATS THE JOB WITH CARE.

AS AFFABLE AS THEY COME, TOO.
HELPS WHEN WE CHECK OUT A SCENE. GETS PEOPLE TALKIN'.
LISTENS TO EVERY VICTIM LIKE A SAINT.
NOT EVEN I CAN GET PEOPLE TO SING LIKE HE DOES.
NO WONDER. YOU'RE THE "BAD COP."
THAT GUY REALLY LOVES PEOPLE.
THAT'S-- I GUESS YOU COULD SAY...
THAT'S KUJOH'S TALENT.
I TELL YA...

I'D BE IN A REAL FIX IF HE QUIT.
FOR THE FIRST TIME, WE AGREE ON SOMETHING.
HUH? WHAT I'M SAYIN' IS...
IT'D BE A NASTY SURPRISE AFTER I TURNED DOWN THIS JOB IN OSAKA!
WHADDA YOU KNOW?!
GRR... GRR...
HEAR THAT?
THAT'S GREAT NEWS, MR. KUJOH!

GUH...
PLIP...
のそ...
SOB
SOB
SOB
SOB
BUH... I...
WHAT'S THIS UTTER HOGWASH?!
I REALLY THOUGHT...
I THOUGHT...
SNIFF
YOU'D GIVEN UP ON ME...
SO!
AS FOR THIS RECIPE...
TAPIOCA PUDDING
Top secret

IT'S THE PUDDING THEY MAKE HERE, RIGHT?
MHM. AND THE HAND-WRITING ON THE ENVE-LOPE IS THE SAME AS ON THE MENU.
WHY? BECAUSE IT'S SHINDOH'S FATHER'S.
READ CAREFULLY! -SHINDOH
HIS FATHER'S ?!
NEWHALL DINER
OF COURSE! THE CURRY'S FROM KANSAI, LIKE SHINDOH.
AND "NEW HALL" IS JUST "SHINDOH" IN ENGLISH.
HE MIGHT JUST HAVE BEEN A TAD TOO EMBAR-RASSED TO TELL YOU.
Well, this youngster workin' for Eiji...
He's real fond of our house puddin'.
HEAD CHEF MR. SHINDOH
So, my boy had me give him the recipe.
Said he wanted to commemorate the kid's first undercover job!

Wanted to make him some puddin'.
YOU LIKE MAKING DESSERT?!
THAT'S SO NEAT!
SHUT UP.
IS MR. HARD-BOILED BLUSHING?
WHAT A FANCY MAN!
TCH!
KUJOH!
SHYEAH? SIR!
I KNOW I SAID I'D BE IN A FIX WITHOUT YOU.

BUT IF YA EVER DO WANNA CALL IT QUITS...
JUST TALK TO ME. DON'T BRING IT TO THESE BOZOS.
I KNOW MY LIMITS.
I DON'T GET PEOPLE'S FEELINGS LIKE YOU DO.
SO YOU GOTTA *TELL* ME.
AND I'LL HANDLE IT PROPERLY.
GOT IT?
YES, SIR.
MR. SHINDOH?

I COULDN'T HAVE ASKED FOR A BETTER BOSS.
THAT'S GOIN' A BIT FAR.

WHO WANTS SOME SUPER SPECIAL PUDDIN'?
EIJI'S TREAT! ♪
...
YAY!
CASE 14 CLOSED

CASE 15
OH, MIMI!! ♪
IT'S YOUR FAVORITE TIME OF DAY!
SNACK TIME!
Madeleine
...
NO THANKS.
WHAT?!

WHY?
YOU'RE ALWAYS FATTENING ME UP.
I TRIED TO PUT ON A DRESS THIS MORNING, AND IT DIDN'T FIT ANYMORE...
THEN THIS MADELEINE FROM NIS-SHINDOH SHALL ENTER MY STOMACH. ♡
YOINK
YOU'D LOOK GOOD ANY WHICH WAY. ♡
EAT WHAT YOU WANT! ♡
THE ISSUE IS HOW *I'D* FEEL ABOUT IT.
DID I HEAR THAT SOMEONE'S HAVING WEIGHT TROUBLES?
SWOOF
IN THAT CASE...
DO I EVER HAVE THE CURE FOR YOU!

CASE 15
Scarlet Fingertips
(Part 1)

ALLOW ME TO INTRODUCE MYSELF.
MY NAME IS TANABE. I'M WITH KOHMORIDOH PHARMACEUTI-CALS.
PERHAPS YOU'VE HEARD OF OUR WARES!
A SALES-MAN?
HE'S TODAY'S CLIENT.
OUR BEAUTY PRODUCTS ARE *FLYING* OFF THE SHELVES.
That's right; it's no mere quackery!
HAIR RECOVERY
and even arm hair.
have never known
such smoothness.
HAIRY?
WE'RE FAMED FOR FAST RESULTS!
THIS WEIGHT LOSS TONIC IN PARTICULAR!
Ridiculed for corpulence? Restore your Slender Figure
MEN & WOMEN

IT'S A HIT WITH MEN AND WOMEN OF ALL AGES!
NOW THAT YOU MENTION IT, I'VE SEEN THIS AD FREQUENTLY.
KRSH
YOU SHOULD TRY IT OUT!
SO? WHAT DO YOU NEED FROM US?
OH, WOULD YOU HEAR ME OUT?
YEP. IT'S OUR JOB.
WELL, WE PUT UP SOME POSTERS ADVERTISING THIS PRODUCT IN TOWN...
BUT LAST WEEK, SOMEBODY TORE THEM DOWN!

Ridiculed for corpulen
Restor
Slender
Your sa
Kohmoridon's
eight loss
ic
MUST BE BECAUSE WE USED THAT ONE LADY'S PICTURE.
EITHER IT'S SOME MAN WHO FELL HEAD OVER HEELS FOR HER...
OR SOME WOMAN WHO WAS SHORT ON LOOKS, AND OUR PRODUCTS DIDN'T HELP.
WE OCCASIONALLY GET COMPLAINTS LIKE THAT.
AWFUL, DON'T YOU THINK?
NOW! HOW'S ABOUT A SAMPLE?
I KNEW HE WAS HERE TO SELL!
男女
ふ
せ
薬
THAT'S TORN DOWN, ALL RIGHT.

OSMETICS
DRUG STORE
FRACTAL
LOOKS LIKE THE OTHER ADS ARE UNSCATHED, THOUGH.
HAVE YOU SEEN ANYTHING?
DRUG STORE
FRIEND Sanitary Shields
POTENT COUGH SYRUP
SOFT CURD
SHOP-KEEPER #1
IT WAS A WOMAN, ACCORDING TO MY WIFE.
SHOP-KEEPER #2
WHEN I YELLED AT HER TO STOP, SHE UP AND RAN AWAY!
REDDISH-BROWN HAIR, SHE HAD.
MIGHT HAVE BEEN A FOREIGNER.
SHOP-KEEPER #3
IT WAS A DEMON, I TELL YOU!
HER FINGERS WERE RED! SOAKED WITH ***BLOOD!***
I JUST KNOW IT.

IT WAS THE UGLY HAG FROM THE UNDER-WORLD--THE YOMOTSU-SHIKOME!
KOJIKI
SO NOW WE'RE CHASING A DEMON?
EVERYONE AGREES THAT IT WAS A WOMAN, AT LEAST.
WE'RE NOT A LIBRARY, YOU KNOW.
AH, ER, RIGHT!
I SUP-POSE...
BUT IT'S STRANGE--WITH SO MANY WITNESSES, WHY HASN'T SHE BEEN CAUGHT BY NOW?
ぽすんっ
BOFF
I'LL HAVE THIS ONE AS WELL!
LADY

TAIUNDOH
CLASSIC LITERATURE COLLECTIONS
SO THIS IS WHAT YOU LIKE TO READ! ♡
LADY
IF IT REALLY WAS BLOOD, WE COULD HAVE A CRIME ON OUR HANDS.
AS MUCH AS I'D HATE TO, WE *COULD* ASK SHINDOH AND HIS GANG...
MUH...
MIMI!
BLOODY FINGERS, RIGHT?

FOR A NATURAL BLACK LUSTER
For gray and sun-bleached hair
ACCENT YOUR NAILS
A sign of hygiene and beauty, well-groomed nails announce your elegance and intellect.
DAZZLE WITH SCARLET RED NAIL ENAMEL
• Liquid Polish
• Powder Polish
• Polish Paste
COULD SHE HAVE MEANT...
THIS?
RED NAIL

THIS IS NAIL ENAMEL, A NEW PRODUCT.
IT WENT ON SALE ONLY THREE DAYS AGO.
THREE DAYS?!
TO MY UNDERSTANDING, YES.
ALLOW ME TO CONFIRM.
MAYBE IT *WAS* A DEMON, THEN...
HMM.
DON'T BE CHICKEN!
WE CAN AFFORD IT IF WE POOL OUR MONEY TOGETHER!
I GUESS ...
WHAT ARE YOU HESITATING FOR?!

Ridiculed for corpulence?
Restore your
lender Figure
our savior, Kohmoridoh's weight loss tonic
YOU SEE WHAT IT SAYS HERE?
WE NEED MEDICINE TO TREAT THIS.
OR DO YOU WANT PEOPLE TO KEEP TALKING BEHIND YOUR BACK?
GOD, I HATE THAT STUPID AD.
IS THAT WHY YOU WERE SO CURT WITH THE CLIENT?
SO YOU NOTICED ...
WE HAVE TO TREAT OUR CLIENTS EQUALLY.
MIMI...
DON'T YOU THINK IT'S STRANGE?

IF ANYONE SHOULD CHANGE, IT'S NOT THE PERSON WHO'S *BEING* BULLIED.
AND EVEN IF YOU ATTAIN "BEAUTY"...
IT'S NOT LIKE THAT'LL STOP PEOPLE FROM GOSSIPING ABOUT YOU.
There he goes again.
What is he, a handbag boy?
RIGHT...
OF COURSE.
SAKU'S HAD TO ENDURE A LOT OF ABUSE.

HE'S FINALLY LEARNED TO SPEAK HIS MIND...
?
POOR THING.
LISTEN TO ME PRATTLE, HA HA!
I WONDER WHAT OUR YOMOTSU-SHIKOME'S MOTIVATIONS WERE.
I'M STARTING TO FEEL LIKE THAT DESERVES SOME THOUGHT.
DETEC-TIVES!
THANK YOU FOR WAITING!
ABOUT THE NAIL ENAMEL...

IT SEEMS THAT BEFORE REACHING DEPARTMENT STORES, IT WAS SOLD TO MANICURISTS.
MANI-CURISTS, YOU SAY?
WELCOME!

GAWP
たじっ
UPSCALE BARBER-SHOPS HAVE MANICURISTS NOWADAYS!
I GET MY NAILS TRIMMED HERE MYSELF.
UH-HUH!
SPARKLE
SPARKLE
ARE MOST OF YOUR CLIENTELE MEN?
THAT'S RIGHT.
I'D SAY THE MAJORITY'S MEN PREPARING FOR A DANCE.
HMM...
WELL THEN. YOUR HAND, PLEASE.
A STYLISH LADY DETECTIVE LIKE YOU...
SURELY YOU'RE INTERESTED?

PUH...
PRETTY ...
I THINK I'LL TAKE ONE...
IT'S TOTALLY YOUR STYLE!
CERTAINLY! THANK YOU FOR YOUR PURCHASE.
BUT THIS JUST MAKES IT ALL THE MORE CONFUSING.
IF THE "RED FINGERS" *WAS* THIS ENAMEL...
SHE'D HAVE TO BE *IN THE KNOW* TO GET IT SO SOON.
SO OUR DEMON'S STAYING AHEAD OF THE TRENDS!
RIGHT. AND THERE'S ONE MORE THING.
ALL THE DRUG STORES THAT WERE HIT?
THEY'RE CONCENTRATED IN ONE AREA.
LET'S SEE, WHAT ELSE IS AROUND THERE...

THUNK
THE IMPERIAL UNIVER-SITY!
I'M OFF TO TAKE A FEW STATE-MENTS!
WHA--?
BUT I'M NOT FINISHED YET!
WAIT HERE! I'LL JUST BE A MOMENT!
MA'AM! WAIT!
AW, COME ON...
MIMI...

A BROWN-HAIRED LADY?
REMOVING POSTERS?
HOW CURIOUS...
PERHAPS JOIN US INSIDE AND WE CAN--
NO, NO! THANK YOU FOR YOUR ASSISTANCE!
ACK!
PHEW...
EXCUSE ME.
WHOOSH...

I BELIEVE ...
I MIGHT KNOW THE PERSON YOU'RE LOOKING FOR.
REALLY ?!
YES.
SHE'S OVER THIS WAY.
COME WITH ME.
...
HRM...

SOME-
THING'S
FISHY
HERE.
HE WON'T LOOK ME IN THE EYES-- NOT EVEN SHOW HIS FACE.
PERHAPS I SHOULD GO GET SAKU...
WE'RE HERE.
SHE'S INSIDE.
SHABBY
...
IS SOME-
THING THE MATTER?
ACTU-
ALLY...
COULD YOU WAIT HERE FOR A MOMENT?

A FRIEND'S WAITING FOR ME NEARBY.
I'LL BE BACK IN JUST--
SMAK
COME.
HUH?
WAIT A MOMENT.
WHAT ARE YOU--

WOULD YOU STOP IT?!
OH?
RED AS A ROSE...

GET IN.

WOW! SO NEAT AND TIDY...
NO! I DON'T HAVE TIME FOR THIS!
HOW MUCH DO I OWE YOU?!
PAYING FOR MITSUKO AS WELL.
YOU SEEM TO HAVE AN EXCITING JOB!
SURE... THOUGH I HAVE SOME TROUBLE KEEPING UP...
MY BOSS IS A REAL LIVE WIRE...
HEE HEE.
YOU'RE NOT RELYING ON ME AT ALL, MIMI.
DID YOU FORGET ALREADY?

I'M YOUR ASSISTANT AND BODYGUARD!
CASE 15 GOES ON

CONTINUED IN VOL 4

Bartholomew & Mitsuko

IT CAN BE PAINFUL TO SEE YOURSELF IN SOMEONE ELSE.

THE PRIVILEGED CLASS

AS FOR SHINDOH

Special

Thanks!

MY DEEPEST GRATITUDE
GOES OUT TO:
KON-CHAN
HARUKA-CHAN
ALL THE DESIGNERS AND BOOKSTORES
MY EDITOR AND THE WHOLE
EDITORIAL DEPARTMENT
AND EVERYONE ELSE WHO AIDED IN
THE PUBLISHING OF THIS BOOK.

IN THE NEXT VOLUME...

Mitsuko trapped...

A mysterious student with something to hide...

Tu es
ma détective
chérie

Natsumi Ito
Presents

The Masterful Cat is Depressed Again Today
1
Story and Art by Hitsuzi Yamada
A Story of Seven Lives
story & art by Shirakawa Gin
EX-YAKUZA & STRAY KITTEN
1
STORY AND ART BY RIDDLE KAMIMURA
THE EVIL SECRET SOCIETY OF CATS
1
STORY & ART BY PANDANIA
Creepy Cat
story and art by COTTON VALENT
vol.1
YOKAI CATS
1
STORY & ART BY PANDANIA

01
story and art by
I Am a
Cat Barista

1
story & art by
Haru
Hisakawa
MANAGER
Cat
Massage
Therapy

My Sister, the Cat
1
story & art
Senko

Wonder Cat
Kyuu-chan 1
Story & Art by Sasami Nitori

STORY & ART BY
Konomi Wagata
my NEW Life as a Cat
1

MY DEAR DETECTIVE
MITSUKO'S CASE FILES

MY DEAR DETECTIVE: MITSUKO'S CASE FILES VOL. 3
STORY AND ART BY NATSUMI ITO

First published by Futabasha Publishers Ltd., in 2021
English version published by Seven Seas Entertainment, Inc.

Translation: **Samuel R. Messner**
Lettering: **Rina Mapa**
Cover Design: **H. Qi**
Proofreader: **Krista Grandy**
Production Designer: **Ria Linn Johnson**
Quality Control: **Reid Urchison**
Editor: **Nick Mamatas**

Seven Seas Entertainment, Inc. | President: **Jason DeAngelis** | Vice President: **Adam Arnold** Publisher: **Lianne Sentar** | Licensing Managers: **Y. Takahashi & Lena LeRay** | Licensing Associate: **Cheryl Ng** | Editor-In-Chief: **Julie Davis** | Managing Editors: **Jack Sullivan & Shanti Whitesides** Production Manager: **John Ramirez** | Assistant Production Manager: **Jinky Besa** | Materials Associate: **Jill Sanogal** | Prepress Technicians: **Salvador Chan Jr., April Malig, & Jules Valera** Digital Operations Manager: **CK Russell** | Digital Contents Manager: **Kristine Johnson** Administrative Associate: **Danya Adair** | Inventory & Logistics Manager: **Marsha Reid** | Sales & Marketing Manager: **Lauren Hill** | Marketing Associates: **Leanna Cruz & Ryley Moore**

ISBN: 979-8-89160-755-2
Printed in Canada
First Printing: June 2025
10 9 8 7 6 5 4 3 2 1